TOM STETSON

and the

Giant Jungle Ants

By

JOHN HENRY CUTLER

Illustrated by

URSULA KOERING

★

WHITMAN PUBLISHING COMPANY
RACINE, WISCONSIN

CONTENTS

"Uncle Leo, See That Smoke!"

TOM STETSON
and the
Giant Jungle Ants

CHAPTER ONE

JUNGLE TRAIL

Tom Stetson stood on the deck of his uncle's launch and scanned the shore through binoculars. He could hardly believe his eyes. Smoke was curling from the dense green jungle his missionary uncle had told him was uninhabited.

"Uncle Leo, come quick!" he shouted. "I'm sure I see smoke rising over the treetops a few miles inland."

One week in Brazil was enough to convince Tom that he was in a land of wonders. His uncle, Leo Jason, who was a medical missionary, had invited him to spend his summer vacation cruising on the Amazon River, its tributaries, and the muddy inland jungle streams where he made stops at Indian settlements, and Tom had jumped at the chance. Tom was an ordinary American youngster in the third year of high school. He liked adventure, the more daring the better! As he handed the binoculars to his uncle he had a feeling that he would not have long to wait.

9

Uncle Leo's puzzled expression meant that something was brewing.

The missionary's tanned face still had a tense, wondering look as he peered through the binoculars. "It beats me," he said, half to himself as he handed the glasses back to Tom. "I've been patrolling the Amazon Basin and many unexplored places in Brazil for more than twenty years, and this is the first time I've ever seen any sign of human life in this region. We're really on the ragged edge of nowhere, lads."

He turned to Manolo, an Indian youngster, who, like Tom, was in his early teens. Leo Jason had adopted Manolo eleven years earlier when the Indian was three or four years old. He had found the sad-faced child in an abandoned settlement not far from the headwaters of the Xingu River where head-hunters and other wild savages roamed. Manolo, he knew, belonged to one of the primitive tribes haunting the rain-soaked forest in that uncharted region, but Mr. Jason had never been able to find out which one, for Manolo could speak only a few words when he was found.

Tom, now more excited than alarmed, saw the intent look that crept into Manolo's usually calm, bronze features as he trained the glasses on the black smoke curling up toward the tropical blue sky. Manolo returned the binoculars to Mr. Jason without saying a word. The husky youngster seldom spoke unless he had something important to say.

"Haul the skiff alongside, Manolo," the missionary said quietly as he kept his eyes glued on the curling smoke. "We're going ashore to see what's going on back there. It looks to me as though some savage tribe has set up housekeeping."

The missionary's forty-foot motor launch, the *Paloma*, had a shallow draft that enabled it to skirt the shore, but years of experience had taught him to keep it anchored beyond the range of Indian arrows, spears and blowguns. The *Paloma*, which was powered by twin Diesel engines, was moored about half a mile off shore in a muddy inlet a few miles southwest of the juncture of the Amazon and the Tapajos Rivers.

Tom gazed dreamily at the gigantic wilderness sprawled out before them. Here he was, in plain view of an unmapped jungle, on the threshold of the largest remaining unexplored area in the world. In that jungle were birds of brilliant plumage and snakes of every description and size. Here were the uncontrolled forces of the untamed wilderness. Tom thought of the huge cockroaches he had seen in a native hut in Belem—those disgusting-looking vermin, some of which were four inches long. He remembered how frightened he had been when he had first set eyes on them as they scampered around the dirt floor among the lizards. But what were those roaches compared with the wild animals he would soon see in the jungle?

"Don't make any unnecessary noise, boys, when we go ashore," Mr. Jason warned as they hopped into the skiff. Tom could feel his heart pounding like a triphammer against his chest, but he tried to appear calm and casual.

"I won't crack a twig, Uncle Leo," he said.

As the skiff shot through the muddy water, gliding swiftly over the placid surface under Manolo's smooth strokes, Tom sat stiffly in the stern. How different was this inland waterway from the blue-green ocean lapping Cape Cod, he thought, as he glanced over his shoulder at the wake left by the craft. He wished Manolo or his uncle would say something— something cheerful and reassuring. But the Indian youngster was silent and sphinx-like as usual, and the usually relaxed missionary, who was sitting in the bow, kept his eyes intently fixed on the shore. A few minutes later Manolo guided the skiff into a little cove. Tom helped him drag the boat ashore and secure it firmly to the trunk of a tree as Mr. Jason looked for a trail. There was something awe-inspiring about the wild beauty of the surroundings. The almost impenetrable wilderness which lined the shore was a deep green. As he gazed up at the towering trees he noticed that they were connected by twisting vines of varying thickness, and the space between the trees was full of all kinds of shrubbery. His eye ran up the perpendicular trunk of a coconut palm to the drooping branches swaying gently in the breeze. It looked like a mammoth umbrella.

The deep silence was broken now and then by the twittering notes of some birds mingled with the mournful notes of others, and above the slight rustle of the wind he could hear the distant howling of monkeys. He glanced toward the dimly lit jungle. Here he was, a young high school student who had spent most of his life in a city or at a seashore, about to enter that mysterious untraveled region. "Many a missionary and explorer has gone into the uncharted backlands of Brazil and has never returned to tell the story," his uncle had told him. And yet he did not dread the prospect. He felt a yearning to see the animals he could hear howling. What kind of bird was making that throaty, discordant sound? And would they hear the blood-curdling yells of savage Indians, whose life had never before been disturbed by white men? And just what kind of human beings inhabited this equatorial region?

"Okay, lads, follow me in single file," Uncle Leo suddenly called as he thrust a branch aside. "I think I've found a hunter's trail."

Tom's heart skipped a beat as he brought up the rear, walking warily along the narrow, twisting, dimly lit trail. The forest pathway was almost completely arched overhead by the spreading branches. The scattered rays of sunshine that filtered through danced on the walls of foliage and bounced off into darkness. A short distance up the trail they came to a fork. They stopped beneath a Brazil nut tree about seventy feet tall. Tom looked up at the clusters of nuts in pods as large as footballs. He knew that each brown shell contained from twelve to twenty of the three-cornered nuts, neatly packed together, but this was the first time he had seen any of them.

"We'd better not stand under those Brazil nuts, boys," the missionary said as he surveyed the place where the trail forked in two directions. "If one of those nuts hits you on the head you might get a concussion."

"How do the natives pick them, Uncle Leo?" Tom asked curiously. "Do they shinny up the trees?"

"Oh, no. That's not necessary, Tom," Mr. Jason answered, still debating as to which path they would follow. "The shells get so heavy they fall to the ground, and the natives simply pick them up. But they hold wooden shields over their heads while collecting them to keep from getting hurt."

Manolo, who had advanced a few yards up the left trail, returned and shook his head. "Nobody in sight," he said simply.

"Well, maybe we'd better take the trail to the

right that runs parallel, or roughly parallel, to the river, boys," Mr. Jason said. "We'd better not get too close to that smoke until we see what we're up against. And I reckon we can put away our machetes, now. This path is fairly well worn. And it beats me. I haven't been around here for a couple of years, I'll admit, and I've never come ashore in this vicinity, but I still feel pretty sure that no Indians have been living around here very long."

The thick jungle walls flanking the trail drowned out the faraway howling of the monkeys, but brightly colored birds that flew from bough to bough filled the wilderness with music, and hundreds of insects could be heard buzzing in every clump of foliage. The steaming air was heavy with odors that ranged from perfume to the sickening smell of rotting vegetation. And the ground was covered with ants.

"Gosh, the air in this jungle tunnel is enough to make you sick," Tom murmured as he mopped his brow with his handkerchief.

"Well, Tom, it would be a lot worse if it weren't for those ants you see crawling all over the place. By eating everything in their path they keep the vegetation from decaying more than it would normally. In regions where the ants are scarce the smell is sometimes nauseating."

"Well, I guess it works both ways, Uncle," Tom

said as they headed leisurely up the trail. "They ruin gardens and orchards, too, don't they? And don't they often strip trees of their leaves?"

"I'll say they do, Tom. Turn around and walk back in the direction we came for about twenty yards and you can see an army of ants doing a job on a cannon-ball tree."

"That's a strange name for a tree," Tom said excitedly as they retraced their steps. He had heard of the tree ants which were capable of ruining the most majestic growths. And now he would see them.

"I wait here," Manolo smiled as he folded his arms and leaned against a tree. "Ants too boring."

"Not for me, Manolo, old boy," Tom shot back over his shoulder as he hurried after the missionary. They stopped near a tree that was covered with red blossoms.

"See why it's called a cannon-ball tree, Tom?" his uncle asked. "Its fruits look just like round cannon balls, don't they?"

"Boy, you can say that again, Uncle. But those flowers growing on the tree are beautiful."

"And I might add that sometimes the fruit you see sounds like a cannon ball when it bursts during high winds."

"And, jumping Jupiter, Uncle! Look at that procession of ants going up the tree. And on the opposite side another file of ants is coming down carrying pieces of leaves. What a system!"

"Come over here and you'll see something else, Tom. See those ants stationed up in the tree? They are the cutters. Their job is to bite off the stems of the leaves, and when they fall to the ground, another ant troop cuts up the leaves so they'll be easier to carry."

Tom was fascinated as he watched another long single file of ants taking the tiny pieces of leaves away. As he followed his uncle toward Manolo, who led the way as soon as they had caught up with him, Tom could see huge moths and butterflies flitting over their heads and disappearing into the underbrush. Everything was wild and huge and uncontrolled here in the jungle! There, on the left, were strange-looking tropical plants with leaves fifteen inches wide. Strange-looking growths were clinging to the trunks of the trees, and unfamiliar birds and insects could be seen from time to time. It was just like walking through a museum—a dark narrow museum with a roof of branches.

A creaking of branches and twigs interrupted Tom's train of thought. As he glanced in the direction of the sound he saw, to his horror, that Manolo had disappeared.

"Well, I'll be—Manolo. What happened, Uncle? He disappeared right into the ground." Tom stood frozen in his tracks as the missionary rushed for-

ward. His eyes and mouth were opened wide, and
he could feel his mouth going dry as he clasped and
unclasped his hands. He remembered how he had
once sunk up to his armpits in quicksand, and the
agonizing sensation he had experienced then returned to him now. He inched forward numbly toward his uncle who was kneeling down resting on
his hands.

"Manolo has fallen into a pit, Tom, but don't
worry. We'll get him out. South American Indians
often dig these deep pits around their camps to trap
animals for food or any approaching enemy, especially hostile Indian rivals. Notice the mud-caked
walls. When the clay around here dries it gets so
slippery it's impossible for a person to climb out
unaided."

In the dim shadows of the round pit, about eight
or nine feet in diameter, Tom could barely see Manolo's head bobbing about as he tried to get a foot-
hold on the almost perpendicular walls.

"Take it easy, Manolo, old boy," Tom whispered.
"We'll have you out of there in a jiffy."

Tom watched his uncle cut a thick liana vine with
his razor-sharp machete and drop one end of the
vine down to Manolo. "Okay, Tom, let's heave-ho,"
he said. A moment later Manolo, still calm and unafraid, was standing beside them.

"Many thanks." He smiled, and his white teeth

shone in his dark face.

"We'd better cover this pit so the Indians won't know we've been around," Mr. Jason said.

When they finished putting the leaves and branches back in place Tom grinned at his uncle. "I don't think those Indians could have done a neater job of camouflaging," he said.

"Let that be a lesson to you, lads," Mr. Jason warned as they threaded their way along the trail. "There may be more traps."

"Say, Uncle," Tom whispered a few seconds later, "I see footprints of some kind in the clay. They look as though they were made by human feet except for those deep imprints where the big toe should be."

"Nice snooping, Tom!" his uncle whispered back. "But I don't understand. It's very strange. The only Indians I know of who leave tracks like those are the Motilon Indians who make life miserable for white folk in the backlands of Venezuela. Very strange, very strange—"

"But what about the big toes, Uncle?" Tom asked.

"That's what I mean. The Motilon holds his bow with his big toe when he shoots arrows. As a result, his big toes—both of them—are bent almost at right angles. I was dead sure there were none of those murderers in this neck of the woods. But whoever these Indians around here are, I'm just as certain I've never run across them before."

"I never heard of anyone shooting arrows with their feet, Uncle. How—"

"Well, Tom," the missionary interrupted, "when a Motilon draws a bead on an animal or a human, he sits down, places his big toes against the bow, and pulls the bowstring with both hands. The arrows, which travel at a terrific speed, are amazingly accurate." He paused for a moment to note their position in the jungle. "We'd better hurry, Tom. We're falling behind Manolo. One of my friends once told me he saw an employee of an American oil company shot through the chest with one of their arrows, which are barbed, by the way. Nobody saw the Motilon shoot, but later his tracks were found about ninety yards away."

"Boy, it's hot today," Tom said, as he mopped his brow. "This is no day for tramping in the jungle. How did they know it was a Motilon who shot the arrow?"

"There were several clues," Mr. Jason said as they caught up with Manolo. A heavy undergrowth screened them on both sides, and they could no longer see the river as the trail wound up a gradual slope. "One clue was the footprints, which were just like the ones we saw back there. Another was the smell of alligator grease which all Motilon males plaster on their skin to ward off mosquitoes. And the arrow was made of black palm, one of the hardest woods known, although not so hard or heavy as the ironwood that grows around here. Their bows, by the way, were six feet long."

"Hope we never run into any of those Indians," Tom said. "They sound a lot more dangerous than the North American Indians used to be."

"They are." Mr. Jason stopped for a moment. "Slow down, Manolo," he said. "Remember I'm almost fifty-seven." Manolo smiled apologetically and suited his pace to Mr. Jason's. Turning to Tom again, Mr. Jason continued. "The Motilons are so deadly the employees of the oil companies in Venezuela wear bulletproof vests. Some even wear armor, and only a fool would go around in Motilon territory unarmed. No Motilon has even been known to attack a person who has firearms. Those devils are never seen when they trail a victim. They slither through the underbrush without breaking a twig. Okay, Manolo, keep going."

"You mean they can come within arrow's range without being seen or heard?" Tom asked.

"Righto, Thomas. And like most South American Indians, they don't need a compass. They know that all trees bend toward the south in the jungle, and that the branches on that side are stronger and the bark thicker than on the north side. When one of my missionary friends gave a Motilon a compass he used it as a toy."

"Gosh, Uncle Leo, right this minute we may be being watched by some of them. What a scary thought!" Tom glanced cautiously at their surroundings, but discovered nothing remotely resembling a Motilon.

"It's possible," the missionary said as he increased his pace to keep up with Manolo, "but I doubt it. We're quite a distance from Venezuela, and those Motilons, as far as I know, stay in their home territory. But I'd certainly like to know what tribe has moved in around here. I reckon there'd still be plenty to learn if I lived in Brazil a hundred years. I wonder where these footprints lead."

"Here's another set of footprints," Tom exclaimed. "The set we've been following was made by someone coming from the direction of the pit Manolo fell into. This second set of prints was made by an Indian who belongs to the same tribe. They seem to have met right at this spot," he said pointing down to the ground, "and then one Indian followed the other."

"Wait a minute, Manolo," the missionary said in a low tone. "Well, Tom, I can see that your boy scout training has made you jungle wise. As far as I can see, you've hit the nail right on the head. The second Indian broke through the underbrush at this spot."

"You think maybe they see the *Paloma?*" Manolo

"They Seem to Have Met Here."

suddenly asked. It was the second time he had spoken since Tom first spied the smoke from the launch.

Mr. Jason looked worried. "I guess," he said slowly, "that's a chance we'll have to take. These tracks are fresh. We might have been spotted from the river's edge if the Indians were down there in the past couple of hours. Let's follow the tracks for a while and see where they lead. I have a hunch that the two Indians who made these tracks are hunting for food. And I'll wager their footprints will lead us to other pits."

The trail was narrow, but well worn and easy to follow.

"I'm glad it leads away from the clump of bushes where we hid the skiff in case we have to make a quick getaway," Tom said. "Wonder why Manolo stopped, Uncle?"

Manolo pointed to the ground without speaking until they caught up with him. "More trap," he said.

"Why, there's a hole in the covering of leaves and branches," Tom whispered breathlessly. "Something must have fallen through."

"Let's listen a minute," Uncle Leo whispered. "Either there's something in there or the Indians did a punk job of camouflaging their trap this time."

The silence of the jungle was unbroken except by the constant buzzing of insects and the occasional cry of a bird or howl of a monkey. Mr. Jason cautiously lifted some of the branches screening the edge of the pit. In the darkness of the hole a human form was barely visible.

Mr. Jason turned to Tom and Manolo, touching his lips to warn them to make no noise. "There's someone down there, all right." Tom had never seen his uncle so excited. "Stand back while I move away more of these branches so we can see better."

Flat on his stomach, the missionary crawled cautiously forward and pulled away the rest of the branches. He peered into the pit for a brief instant and then, as if startled, drew back quickly and rose to his feet.

"There's a dangerous-looking Indian in there," he whispered. "He's blacked up from head to toe as if he were disguised for night snooping. I have no idea to what tribe he belongs, but I'm dead sure it isn't that mysterious tribe back in there." The missionary waved in the direction from which they had seen the smoke on the *Paloma*.

"You mean," Tom whispered, "he's a captive?"

"Exactly," Mr. Jason said, glancing around to be sure they weren't being watched.

CHAPTER TWO

THE BLACK DUGOUT

"Jeepers, he's black as the ace of spades!" Tom whispered as he gazed at the scowling Indian. "What's that stuff smeared all over him?"

"Mud," his uncle answered. "He plastered himself with mud so he wouldn't be visible at night. He's probably a spy from some enemy tribe. Even his hair is slicked down with mud. I'd sure like to know what tribe he belongs to, and where it is."

"The way he's glaring at us, Uncle! He's just standing there like a sphinx. It kind of makes you shudder the way he keeps showing his teeth and snarling."

"He knows his doom is sealed, and he knows there's nothing he can do about it. There's nothing we can do, either. If we pulled him out of there it might be the last thing we ever did, even though he seems to have been disarmed. He sure has a wicked gleam in his eye."

"Those big toes of his prove he doesn't belong to the same tribe that made the other footprints back there," Tom said. "His aren't bent at right angles."

Manolo pointed to the set of footprints that approached the pit from a direction opposite the other two sets. "He come this far and fall," he said.

"We'd better return to the *Paloma* for the present," Mr. Jason said as he led the way back. "In this case discretion is better than valor. Later we'll set up an attraction post near the river, and if the Indians up in the hills accept our peace offerings we can make the next move."

"What's an attraction post?" Tom asked as he tried to keep close to the missionary.

"You'll see very soon, Tom. I always set one up when I try to convert the Indians if they've never been contacted by missionaries before."

As they swiftly retraced their steps toward the skiff, Mr. Jason paused now and then as a shadow darkened the trail when an anteater or a tiny spider monkey crossed it and darted into the woods.

"Those little animals sure are cute," Tom said, "but I'd like to know what those other animals are I can hear rustling through the jungle."

"Could be anything from a tapir to a jaguar," Mr. Jason said as he held a branch to keep it from hitting Tom. "Let's remember to walk around the pit this time, lads. It's just a few yards ahead."

"That attraction post you mentioned, Uncle," Tom said. "When are you going to set it up?"

"Tonight after dark," his uncle replied as they approached the skiff. "We'll erect a crude hut and leave some bright cloth, a machete and a box of salt in it. If the Indians fall for our bait we'll come ashore tomorrow."

Tom and Manolo pushed the skiff into the brown water and all three jumped in. "Here come those thunderclouds," Tom said as he picked up the oars. "The Indians won't be able to see us so well now. Gosh, I've been in Brazil for a week now, and it's poured cats and dogs every day."

"In this part of Brazil it usually rains at least once a day even in the dry season." Mr. Jason smiled. "You should be here'from November to March when it really comes down."

Tom felt his right oar hit something. It was a fish floating on the surface, dead. As the rain came pelting down, dropping like a dark curtain on a bright day, he glimpsed more of the same kind of fish floating belly upward in the coffee-colored water. "Look at those fish," he said. "There are dozens of them floating around."

"There must be some Indians fishing upstream," Mr. Jason said.

"How in the world do you know that, Uncle Leo?"

Mr. Jason reached over the side and picked up a fish that was as long as his forearm.

"This is the way some of the Brazilian Indians catch fish. They stupefy the fish with the ground pulp of a creeper or weed that grows in the jungle. It's called barbasco. They usually pour two or three hundred pounds of the mash into the water and before very long the stupefied fish rise and float belly up. Then the Indians scoop them up with nets at the end of long bamboo handles. It's not very exciting sport, but the Indians are more interested in getting food than in having fun."

"Well," Tom grinned as the skiff glided swiftly toward the *Paloma*, "I'm certainly glad to hear that those Indians in there eat fish. I was afraid they might be cannibals."

"Don't be too sure they aren't cannibals, Tom," the missionary said grimly as they reached the *Paloma*. "Cannibalistic Indians eat fish and all kinds of wild animals. If they had to depend on the human enemies they capture, they'd starve to death. Not many strangers ever get very close to them, remember. Wait until we see what that tribe in there does with the captive Indian we saw in the pit. If they're cannibals, we'll soon know."

"Gosh, Uncle Leo, everything seems so unreal down here in the jungles of Brazil. Just think, we may be the first white men who ever saw this part of the world."

"Right you are, Tom," the missionary said as he slumped onto a canvas chair. All three were soaked when they boarded the launch. After slipping into dry khaki clothes Manolo stretched out on a blanket on the deck and fell fast asleep. The *Paloma* rocked and swayed gently on the coffee-colored river as a soft tropical breeze rippled the water.

As the missionary filled his pipe with tobacco, Tom sat on the deck opposite his uncle and brought his diary up to date. When he finished he noticed that his uncle looked troubled as he glanced toward the curling smoke. The life of a medical missionary was anything but easy, Tom reflected. It was a solitary existence, patrolling the silent backlands of Brazil. There was always the danger of malaria or hookworm or some other disease common in the area near the Equator. And, of course, the jungle was full of wild animals and primitive savages.

A dreamy look came into Tom's eyes as he glanced idly at a large water lily floating a few yards from the *Paloma*. The leaves of the river plant measured almost eight feet in diameter, and it had rims about six inches high. What a living museum Brazil was! He glanced at his watch as the clouds lifted and the blazing sun lit up the afternoon. It was exactly ten minutes past four.

"Gosh, Uncle, I wish I could take a catnap any time like Manolo. But I guess I'm too jittery to be able to snooze now anyway."

"I'm a little jittery myself, as a matter of fact," the missionary said gravely, his gaze still focused on the rolling green jungle. "Ordinarily I have no trouble dropping off to sleep any time, but I feel too concerned about that smoke in there. Maybe it comes from a fire built by an explorer or a *caboclo* who lost his way. It certainly is a puzzle I'd like to solve. I feel it's my duty to investigate things like this and report my findings to the missionary headquarters."

"What about that English explorer you told me about one night in Belem, Uncle? I think you said his name was Colonel Fawcett and that he disappeared a long time ago. Jeepers, it's even possible that he might still be living, isn't it? Maybe he's in there living like a hermit."

Mr. Jason laughed as he shook his head emphatically. "No, Tom, although for many years I had hopes of running across Colonel Fawcett, who vanished under such mysterious circumstances. Years ago he was the big topic of conversation down here, and in the United States and England too, as a matter of fact."

"I never heard of him until you told me about him, Uncle," Tom said as he lay on the deck with his chin cupped in his hands. "When did he disappear?"

"In 1925," his uncle said, settling comfortably in his chair. "He, his son, and another Englishman set out from the last outpost of civilization and headed into an unknown, unexplored region in the Central

Brazilian Plateau. That's the last that was ever heard of any of them, although since then travelers have often claimed that they ran across members of the expedition."

"Jiminy, Uncle. I suppose that nobody will ever know for sure what happened to them. What was Colonel Fawcett looking for?"

"He was looking for what he called a lost world. He sincerely believed that he would find the remains of ruined cities in the interior of the wild region he was penetrating. The general area is known as the *Matto Grosso*, which means big wood. Much of that region is still unexplored, especially around the tributaries of the Amazon west of the Xingu River." He waved toward the jungle that was around them. "That's still virgin territory, too," he said softly. "At least, I thought it was until I saw that smoke."

"Ruined cities in the jungle—what a thought!" Tom said, sitting up and clasping his knees with his hands.

"Well, Tom, it's a matter of historical record that about two centuries ago an expedition consisting of six Portuguese explorers and some Negro slaves and Indian guides made a startling discovery in the interior of the Central Brazilian Plateau. They came across a mountain range, and when they scaled it they found themselves on a grassy tableland on which were the outlines of an ancient city. It was completely deserted, of course. But they saw tremendous blocks of stones and all kinds of buildings and monuments. There were inscriptions on some of the monuments."

Tom's eyes opened wide as he listened spellbound to his uncle's story. "What happened to the people who lived there, Uncle? Were they all killed?"

"Nobody knows, Tom. But the city seemed to have been destroyed by an earthquake. Anyway, Fawcett believed the story, and his chief ambition was to rediscover the lost city. The exploring party also reported that they had found gold coins and mine shafts. They sent word back of their findings, but they never returned to civilization. Nobody knows what their fate was, either. They were either lost or killed. Your guess is as good as anyone else's."

"Gosh, the way expeditions vanish into thin air! I hope we don't disappear like that, Uncle Leo. Tell me more about Colonel Fawcett. Wasn't anything ever heard after he disappeared?"

"Nothing has been heard directly from Colonel Fawcett since May 30, 1925. On that day he sent his last dispatch back to the United States. He said he was penetrating a strange Indian country and that he might not be able to send out any more dispatches. But in 1928 an American exploring party did find some traces of him." The missionary smiled at the rapt look on his nephew's face.

"Come on, Uncle Leo." Tom grinned. "Don't keep me in suspense. What traces did they find?"

"Well, they followed the same trail Fawcett had taken. When they reached a village of the Anauqua Indians the chief's son had a small brass plate hanging around his neck, and it was stamped with the name of a manufacturer that had supplied Colonel Fawcett with some equipment. The chief himself took the expedition to the territory of the Kalapalos Indians, who revealed that they had seen Fawcett and his two companions in 1925. The Kalapalos Indians said that when the party pushed farther into the interior smoke from their fires could be seen for five days as they moved forward. Then, the Indians explained, the party was massacred by some hostile Indian tribe. The Kalapalos tribe blamed the massacre on the Anauquas, but the Anauquas said the real murderers were the Suyá Indians."

"Maybe the Indians were lying, Uncle. Maybe Colonel Fawcett is still alive," Tom said.

"Not much chance of that, my boy. Fawcett was pretty old when he set out on his quest. No, I'm afraid that mystery will never be solved. But as far as the lost city is concerned, I have hopes that someday it will be found. And maybe, when I retire from my missionary work, I'll spend a year or so looking for it. I wouldn't be the least bit surprised but what there are many buried civilizations under the jungles of Brazil. Well, Tom," Mr. Jason smiled. "Does Brazil remind you of Boston?"

Tom rose and walked to the railing on the fantail of the launch. "As far as I can see, Uncle, the only thing Boston and Brazil have in common is a capital B. Wow, what a place, what a place! I've already seen more strange things than I ever thought existed." He sighed as he sat down on a canvas chair. "I wish I didn't have to go back to high school next fall. I like school and football and of course it will be wonderful to see Mom and Pop and the family again, but after all this excitement, life in Boston is bound to seem dull."

"Well, my boy, when you finish school maybe you can come down here and explore places that have never been seen by white men—places, perhaps, that have never been seen by Indians or anyone else, either. I must admit that I have always been intrigued by the thought that I have broken new trails in the world's largest unexplored region. In fact, right now, I'm bursting with curiosity to know more about this wild country right around here. It's always a thrill for me to run across Indian tribes whose existence was never previously known. And there's always something new and different to find in the jungle. Plants that shine at night, for example."

Tom looked at his uncle with a puzzled expression. "Plants that shine at night," he repeated. "Tell me about them."

"Well, there's one kind of fungi that gives off a bluish light at night. It's a strong enough light to read by. And there are other plants almost as remarkable."

"Maybe I'll become an explorer at that, Uncle," Tom said seriously. "Nothing would give me more of a kick. Mom won't want me to be a doctor or a lawyer or an engineer when I tell her about the wonders of Brazil. Wait until she reads about that guan I described in my last letter. She won't believe such a queer-looking bird could exist. Jeepers, imagine a green bird about three feet long, and the way it kept blowing up that pouch under its chin."

"Well, you'll probably see bigger birds than guans before you leave Brazil, Tom. The natives sometimes catch guans with lassos, by the way, and tame them. They make good pets, and they get so fond of their masters they never try to escape. Good eating, too."

"Bigger birds than guans?" Tom asked with mounting interest. He brushed a lock of hair back from his forehead with a quick, nervous gesture.

"Well, you remember the eagles you saw in the cage in the Belem zoo. Then there are huge cranes with big, dangerous bills. I was chased by one of them once. I climbed a Brazil nut tree and finally drove the crane off when I hit it a few times with some of the nut shells. Some of the macaws are as big or bigger than guans, too. Their tails are often more than two feet long, and they are usually beautifully marked with blue and yellow or green and red."

Tom sank into a reverie as his eyes swept the vast tract of jungle. The voyage into the unknown was not far off now. Would they encounter any of the strange sights his uncle had told him about? He had seen thousands of queer-looking animals in the Belem zoo, the best collection of Amazonian wild animals in the world. But it would be so much more fun to see the wild creatures in their native haunts. Maybe they would see a giant eagle swoop down from the sun with its vicious-appearing talons extended. Maybe they would see some of the weird fish that infested the jungle streams. Maybe—

"You seem lost in thought, old boy," Mr. Jason said. "What has impressed you most so far?" The missionary lit his pipe as he glanced at Tom with an amused expression. "Not counting that trip we just made ashore, that is."

Tom pondered the question. "Well, first I thought it was that whopping snake we saw in the zoo—that anaconda. And I was scared out of my wits when I saw that big man-eating alligator in the shallow pool."

"That was a jacare, Tom, not an alligator," the missionary said. "It looks a lot like an alligator or a croc-odile, but it's much more deadly."

"And of course I never saw butterflies on Boston Common with a wingspread of eight or nine inches, Uncle. I never saw such a wide variety of colors either. And that great, big, hairy tarantula you killed on the dock at Santarem was the scariest-looking spider I ever want to see. I never dreamed spiders grew so big."

"Well, Tom, it seems as though everything in Bra-zil grows big. Ants, cockroaches, spiders, worms. Why, there are worms as long as three feet, and some of the anthills could be used as kennels for Great Danes. The rivers are full of river-cows and electric eels several feet long. There are—"

"Electric eels!" Tom gasped. "You mean right around us here there may be electric eels?"

"Yes, indeed," Mr. Jason said quietly. "I've seen so many of them I'm almost bored with the sight of them, but I'm naturally very careful not to get tangled up with them. They're a sort of traveling electric chair."

"I suppose that's how the eels defend themselves, Uncle," Tom said in an awed tone.

"Yes, and that's also how they kill other creatures for food," his uncle said. "They can really dish out a terrific number of volts. Even heavy-mailed alliga-tors and jacares keep clear of electric eels, which, along with the man-eating fish called piranhas, are the rulers of the rivers in Brazil."

Tom glanced down at the muddy stream which harbored so many fascinating creatures. He wondered whether the sea serpents ever swam on the surface of the water. They might be powerful enough to upset the skiff. The idea of eels with electric batteries stirred his imagination.

"The Indians often catch the eels by making them use up their electricity on other animals," the missionary continued. "The eels like to bury themselves in the sand, but they come out at the sound of loud noise and attack the animals the Indians throw into the water. Sometimes monkeys are used. When the eels use up all their electricity they can easily be captured by hand. They grow as long as six or seven feet."

Tom listened breathlessly as the late afternoon breeze freshened. Manolo was still sleeping soundly, and Ozzy was rubbing up against his leg, purring softly. He reached down and picked up the ocelet and stroked its fur.

"You said something about a man-eating fish, Uncle. What's a piranha like?"

"Don't get frightened, now, Tom, if I tell you that right now you are probably within yards of a creature which has often been called the deadliest creature on earth. I wouldn't call it that, but it probably rates as the most dangerous creature as far as human beings are concerned."

Tom's blue eyes widened. He had no idea what his uncle was driving at, and he searched the expression on his face to see if he was teasing him. But the missionary, who still kept glancing thoughtfully toward the smoke that was still rising from the wilderness, had a serious look.

"Why, Uncle, except for you and Manolo and myself the only living thing on the *Paloma* is our pet ocelot, and she's only a pup."

"I don't mean the ocelot. After all, an ocelot is only a spotted cat that belongs to the jaguar family, and Ozzy is as tame as a kitten."

"Well, tell me, Uncle Leo. What do you mean?"

"Piranhas. The gangster fish with the razor-sharp teeth. These inland jungle streams are full of them."

"You mean that little fish I saw in the aquarium in the Belem zoo? The one the keeper fed raw hamburger?"

"Righto, Thomas. A piranha may be less than a foot long, and it may not have teeth as long as sharks, but I'd rather go swimming in water full of sharks than in water full of piranhas."

"You mean to say piranhas are more dangerous than sharks?"

"No. Not singly. But piranhas attack in huge gangs. They are easily aroused by the scent of blood, and they get so wild they often slash one another to shreds. Once I saw a school of piranhas strip an alligator of all its flesh in less than two minutes. Go down to the deep-freeze and get me a small chunk of liver and I'll show you a piranha."

Tom disappeared and was back in a minute. The missionary put the liver on the end of a fishhook and cast the line over the side. "Watch closely, Tom."

A few minutes later Tom saw gleaming white forms gliding swiftly around the surface of the muddy water. Mr. Jason hauled in the line and grabbed a squirming piranha by the tail. It writhed viciously in his tight grip for a moment, baring its sawlike teeth, and finally stopped wriggling.

"Doggone, Uncle, I get what you mean now."

"In Brazil," Mr. Jason said, "you can't be too careful of piranhas and ants. Well, how about a brief siesta? Then we'll have a snack for supper and shove ashore."

The fighting piranha had excited Tom to a point where sleeping was impossible. "I don't feel a bit tired, Uncle Leo," he said: "I think I'll give Ozzy some horse-meat and see if I can pick up anything with the binoculars. I'll have some sandwiches ready for you and Manolo when you wake up."

"All right, Tom. And if you have time, why don't you put a couple of machetes and three or four bandana handkerchiefs in a basket and have them ready. And don't forget the salt. Most Indians would rather have salt than a million dollars. Wake me up around six o'clock, will you?" Mr. Jason retired to the cabin and Tom stayed on deck.

After feeding the affectionate little ocelot, Tom let her cuddle in his lap as he stroked her fur. Then he trained the binoculars on the smoke which could still be seen rising lazily upward against the cloudless sky. Here and there was a splash of bright color as a bird winged its way over the jungle. He saw dozens of ugly black buzzards the size of chickens. He had seen them a few days before in Belem roosting on the huts, waiting for something to die or for some garbage the natives threw in the streets. In some parts of Belem there were no sewers, only great black buzzards with curved beaks.

Suddenly his gaze rested on something long and black. It was being pushed off shore about a mile to the right of the spot where they had rowed ashore a few hours earlier. It was a dugout canoe about thirty or forty feet long. Suddenly several half-naked Indians, painted a bright red, hopped nimbly into it and stood up as they paddled it with broad smooth strokes, one foot resting on the gunwale.

"Uncle Leo!" Tom yelled. "Uncle Leo! Manolo! Wake up, quick! Some Indians are heading right for us, and they're armed with huge bows and arrows!"

CHAPTER THREE

THE ATTRACTION POST

Manolo and Mr. Jason awoke with a start. The missionary looked at Tom with a dazed, drowsy expression as he gathered his wits.

"What was that you said, Tom? Did you say somebody was—"

"Some Indian warriors, Uncle," Tom said frantically, as he waved toward the shore, where the long, black canoe was making good headway. "They're coming toward us, and all of them have bows and arrows. We'd better get underway fast."

Mr. Jason leaped nimbly to his feet, now wide awake. He took in the situation at a glance, but he did not seem disturbed as he turned to Tom.

"Okay, my boy, start the engines. We'd better head downstream and get out of sight. Those Indians in there have spotted us, as I knew they would. In fact, I half planned it that way. All we have to do now is find out whether we're welcome or not. At this point I'd say we were anything but welcome." He smiled. "Those weapons don't look like peashooters."

Tom felt safer when the Diesel engines began to

43

throb. The pursuing Indians, whose swift, smooth strokes had already considerably closed the gap between them and the motor launch, began to whoop angrily as the bow of the *Paloma* swung slowly around. At first the Indians seemed to be gaining as the boat gathered speed. Tom watched their rhythmic strokes as their wooden paddles dipped simultaneously into the river. The narrow canoe drew little water, and it seemed to be skimming the surface with ever-increasing speed as the pursuers tried desperately to overtake the missionary party. They had come to within half a mile of the motor launch when it began to pull away.

The first reaction of the Indians was to increase the tempo of their strokes. They paddled furiously for three or four minutes, until it had become clear that they were losing ground. Then they ceased paddling abruptly, and the two Indians who were sitting forward stood up in the dugout and shot several arrows in the direction of the *Paloma*. In spite of the fact that the arrows fell far short of their mark, they continued to fire them for several minutes.

"What a waste of ammunition," Tom said. "I should think they'd know by now that they couldn't hit us. Shall I keep going at the same speed, Uncle Leo?"

"Yes, Tom. For the moment we might as well let

"What a Waste of Ammunition!"

them think we're leaving for good. Oh, they know very well that they can't hit us, but that's just their way of telling us they don't like us. But they may change their tune when they discover that we mean them no harm. They probably never saw a boat like the *Paloma* before, and they probably never saw white men, either."

"Gosh, what lungs they must have," Tom said. "I never heard anyone yell that loud. But they're turning around now and are heading for shore."

During the whole exciting chase Manolo had remained below, calmly preparing supper, as if nothing were happening. Tom never ceased to wonder at the Indian youngster's coolness and courage. He was always friendly and courteous, but he rarely displayed any emotion. As he guided the *Paloma* around a bend in the stream that had begun to widen, Tom wondered what would become of Manolo. Where would he live after the missionary retired? Could a person like him, who had lived his entire life in the wilds, ever get used to city life? Would he have any desire to go to college, marry and raise a family, or would he spend the rest of his days in the lonely jungle? And what about Uncle Leo? Would he live in Massachusetts when he retired? Tom thought of home now as the delicious aroma of the steak that Manolo was frying drifted up from the galley.

Tom watched his uncle go below to help Manolo with the dinner. It suddenly occurred to him that his uncle and Manolo were closer than even a father and son were ordinarily. The missionary, after all, was the only father Manolo had ever known. The bond between them was so close that they would probably never part company. Wherever the missionary went, the faithful little Indian would follow. He knew that his uncle had spent long hours tutoring his ward, who was no longer a pagan savage, as his tribe had been.

"Okay, Tom, you can drop the hook now," Mr. Jason called from below. "I guess we've gone far enough for the present. And chow is down as we say in the Amazon inland patrol. Come and get it."

"You won't have to invite me twice, Uncle," Tom said cheerily as he shut off the motors and dropped the anchor over the side. "That steak I hear sizzling is making my mouth water."

While they were eating their steak, fried potatoes, canned asparagus and buttered toast, darkness fell without warning, as it does in the equatorial latitudes, where there is almost no twilight and no dawn. They sipped their hot chocolate in the darkness of the deck. Except for the moon that was shining brightly in a cloudless sky, the darkness was complete. Everything was so still and peaceful now, but it had been an eventful day.

"You can help Manolo clean up if you like, Tom, while I head back to our original position. Now that the sun has set those Indians ought to be sound asleep in their hammocks, or wherever they sleep. I don't expect any more trouble from them tonight."

"Gosh, Uncle, these Indians sure lead a healthy life, don't they, hitting the hay so early. I often wondered what savages did at night." Tom paused by the hatchway that opened into the roomy cabin of the *Paloma* as the missionary nosed the craft about.

"Well, they don't always spend their nights so peacefully, Tom," Mr. Jason chuckled. "It depends on what they're up to. If they are warring on another tribe, they are very likely to attack at night."

When Tom and Manolo came up on deck the blurry outline of the shoreline they had visited earlier in the day could be seen in the moonlight. Beyond the trees and jumbled vegetation Tom could see the faint glow of the fire that the Indians kept burning day and night in their settlement. Tom's curiosity, which had been aroused when Manolo brought the skiff alongside, was satisfied when he saw his uncle put a basket of trinkets in the small craft. They were going ashore tonight!

"Well, Uncle Leo!" Tom exclaimed. "I forgot all about the fact that tonight we were going to set up an attraction post."

"I wouldn't dare try to go ashore again in broad

daylight until those Indians become a little friend-lier," the missionary said as he picked up his knap-sack and stepped into the boat. "Do you want to come along?"

"Boy, I'll say I do, Uncle! And look at Ozzy. He seems to want to go, too." Tom hurried below and returned a few seconds later with a bone, which immediately engaged the ocelot's attention. Then he got into the skiff and began to row.

"Head for that clearing over there to the left, Tom," the missionary said. "And we'd better not talk louder than a whisper when we land. We've got to work fast and quietly, because we don't know who may be prowling around. And most Brazilian Indians have very keen hearing."

Tom felt for the first time that he was on the threshold of his first real jungle adventure. They were invading hostile Indian territory where one false move might be fatal. What if the Indians had heard the *Paloma's* motors as they returned? What if they were lurking in the underbrush, waiting to shower them with arrows? It was a scary thought, and the closer they came to the shore, the higher the tension rose.

"Head straight for that little cove, Tom," Mr. Jason whispered.

A moment later they dragged the skiff ashore and pushed their way through the tall vegetation that grew on the river's edge.

"You help Manolo gather some palm leaves, Tom," the missionary said as he set down the basket of peace offerings.

As he collected palm leaves, Tom watched his uncle cut the branch of a tree with his machete and trim it down into a forked pole. He stuck it into the ground and leaned four other poles against the forked end. He secured them with strips of a slender vine which he slashed from a near-by tree. Then he wound vine strips around the crude framework, after which Tom and Manolo piled the palm leaves on them, forming a rough shelter open at one end.

"Get the peace offerings now, Tom, and put them inside," the missionary whispered. "And you can light a small smudge fire, Manolo. Then we'll go back to the *Paloma* and see what happens."

"What's the smudge fire for, Uncle Leo?" Tom asked as Manolo rowed back toward the launch.

"That's to attract the Indians' attention. Otherwise it might be some time before they found the attraction post, and we can't wait around here forever. It might be days or weeks before they wandered down this way."

The day's excitement and the physical exertion had taken their toll on Tom, and now he began to feel weary. He looked forward to a good night's sleep. He yawned as he glanced over his shoulder at

the thick smoke spiraling upward from the fire Ma-
nola had lit. The little Indian had thrown a slow-
burning pulpy wood on the fire that would still be
burning when the Indians awoke at dawn. Then,
when they investigated the fire, things would begin
to happen.

They were about a hundred yards offshore when
a thud was heard near the spot they had just va-
cated. Tom was about to ask what had made the
sound when he heard something whiz through the
air and splash into the water a few yards behind
them.

"They've spotted the fire already," Uncle Leo
said. "Hit those oars, Manolo. Those arrows are getting uncomfortably close."

A third arrow barely grazed the stern of the skiff.
Manolo pulled with all his might. A fourth and a
fifth arrow fell farther behind.

"I think we're out of range now," Mr. Jason said
with a sigh of relief. "Not very chummy, these Indians, are they?"

Manolo let the skiff glide along for a moment as
he raised his oars and cocked his ears. "Hear canoes
go into water," he said. "But maybe we make it."

"Jeepers, I think I can see them shoving the dugouts into the river," Tom cried. "Look! About two
hundred yards to the right of the fire we lit!"

"Three canoes," Manolo said, rowing vigorously.

"Six men in each canoe."

"Gosh, what eyesight and hearing you have, Manolo," Tom said in a tone of admiration. "I'm sure glad we have a couple of hundred yards head start."

"We make *Paloma,*" Manolo said softly. "Unless range of arrow it is too much."

The *Paloma* suddenly loomed up in the moonlight. "While I start her, secure the skiff, Tom," the missionary said. "And you keep your eyes peeled for the dugouts, Manolo."

They quickly boarded their boat, and Mr. Jason hurried to start the engines. "The purr of those engines sounds like sweet music, Uncle Leo," Tom said with a relieved sigh. "Wouldn't it have been awful if they wouldn't start!"

The ping of an arrow slapping the surface of the river interrupted him. It struck a comfortable distance away, but the *Paloma* crew thought of where it might have struck some minutes before.

"Never saw such persistence," Mr. Jason said. "They probably never saw a boat like the *Paloma* before and can't understand why they can't catch us."

"Gee, Uncle, what a day it's been," Tom said as the *Paloma* moved swiftly downstream and away from the shore. "In less than twelve hours we've been chased twice by Indians. Manolo has fallen into one pit, and we saw a wild savage trapped in another. I've seen a piranha, black buzzards, monkeys, anteaters, and beautiful birds. And we don't know who the Indians are who chased us, which adds a bit of spice, huh?"

"Yes, it's been a pretty full day," Mr. Jason said. "I'm glad to see the Indians got discouraged. Whoever they are, we're out of danger now, but we'd better keep moving for a couple of hours."

"Say, Uncle, I meant to ask you before what you meant when you said to watch out for the ants when we go ashore. While we're chugging along, tell me about them, will you, please?"

"Well, Tom," said the missionary tamping down the tobacco in his pipe. "If it wasn't for ants, I might know who Manolo is. You remember I told you that I found him in a deserted Indian camp more than ten years ago. I never told you the camp was deserted quite suddenly because of an ant invasion. The insects drove Manolo's people away, and as far as I know, nobody has ever heard anything about them since."

Tom glanced at Manolo, who was sound asleep. "Imagine not knowing who your people are or where they've gone. Manolo is such a swell kid, Uncle Leo. It doesn't seem fair."

"Yes, Manolo is a fine lad," the missionary said as he sat back on his canvas chair and puffed his pipe slowly. "But it's just as well, perhaps, that he never finds his people. I could tell from their settlement that they were wild and barbaric. I saw piles of monkey skeletons, which means they ate monkeys. Their malokas, or huts, which looked like big beehives, were filthy, and Manolo himself, when I found him, was a little savage. He looked as though he had never heard of soap and water."

"He was just a baby, wasn't he?"

"Yes. Probably about three—maybe four, it's hard to say. All he could say was *hawrapawtaw,* which seems to mean, 'What is that?' That and a few other simple words. I was never able to get very much out of him for the simple reason that he had no idea who he was himself or where he came from."

"You found him near the Xingu River, didn't you?" Tom asked.

"Yes." Uncle Leo settled back comfortably and told his story. "One night I was heading down a narrow jungle stream when I saw a tree covered with old clothes. Ragged loin cloths and plain rags, you understand. Nothing fancy. I had never been in that particular region before, so I stopped at the first native hut I saw. It was a one-room hovel built on stilts about ten feet above the water."

"How did the hut happen to be built on stilts?" Tom asked.

"Well, Tom, you wouldn't have to ask if you ever

saw the Amazon in floodtime. In some places the water rises as much as forty feet when the river overflows its banks and fans out to a width of about four hundred miles in other places. The *caboclos,* or halfbreeds, who are usually a mixture of Indian and Brazilian, even have to build platforms on which to graze their cattle."

"Where do they get the hay or grass if the river rises so much, Uncle?"

"Easy. When the river is low a rich growth of water grass grows to a height of fifteen or twenty feet, and when the river rises this grass is uprooted and drifts downstream."

"Then the *caboclos* haul it over the platforms and feed their cattle?" Tom asked.

"Righto. But I'm getting away from the story of Manolo. When I stopped at the hut the *caboclo* was near death. He told me of the terrible ant invasion that had just passed through the area. He said he had remained neck-deep in a swamp for two days while the terrible column of ants went by. The column was about ten feet wide, he said. He was bitten by so many mosquitoes his face was all puffed up and inflamed."

"Jumping Jiminy, Uncle Leo. How many ants were there, anyway?"

"I have no idea. There must have been millions. I treated the *caboclo* and followed the path of the ants, which had cut a wide swath in the forest, until I came to the Indian settlement. The only person I found there was Manolo. He was curled up in a hammock, fast asleep."

"So you adopted him and named him Manolo."

"Righto. I boarded him in an orphanage in Belem until he was about six. But he was restless there, so I let him come to live with me on the *Paloma*. He's been a big help to me ever since."

"What about those clothes you saw on the tree?"

"When I returned to the *caboclo's* hut I asked him about the clothes. He said he thought the tribe Manolo belonged to put them there, but he knew nothing about the tribe. He was a rubber worker who had just moved to that lonely riverside spot. He was starved when I found him. The ants had eaten all his crops of maize and mandioca. I left him at Belem when I took Manolo there."

"Doggone, Uncle, I see now what you mean about ants. I hope we never run into one of those ant armies."

"I hope we don't, too. The ants are lords of the jungle in Brazil. They are a lot more dangerous than snakes or jaguars. In fact, I know of no animal in the jungle that doesn't make way for the ants."

"What about anteaters?" Tom grinned.

"A good question. But even anteaters would move out of the way if they saw one of those terrible armies approaching, Tom. Well, we'd better turn in. It's almost midnight, and I have a hunch that tomorrow will be even more exciting than today was."

Tom looked up at the stars as his uncle shifted his chair back and yawned. Then, as if what Mr. Jason had said was dawning on him for the first time, he asked, "You mean—you mean we're going back to the place where we've been ducking arrows all day? We aren't even armed!"

CHAPTER FOUR

SIGNS OF FRIENDSHIP

"Why, of course we're going back there, Tom," the missionary said. "It will be interesting to see what happens at the attraction post. If those Indians accept our peace offerings we're going ashore to see what we can do about civilizing them."

The next morning after breakfast Mr. Jason typed a report detailing his medical and missionary activities for headquarters while Tom scanned the mainland. Manolo was dozing in his chair with Ozzy in his lap, blinking in the sunlight. *Good old Manolo,* Tom thought. *He could sleep anywhere, any time.* Tom rose from his chair and began to pace the deck restlessly. Ten minutes past nine. He glanced toward the shore again.

"Somebody is sneaking up to the attraction post, Uncle Leo!" he shouted. Even without the glasses Mr. Jason and Manolo, who had rushed to Tom's side, could see the Indian. He was of average height, clad only in a loincloth. He walked around the attraction post several times without entering it. Then he disappeared into the underbrush.

"He didn't take any of the presents," Tom said.

58

There was disappointment in his voice.

"It's too early to tell anything yet," the missionary said. "I've known Indians to ignore gifts for days, but they usually accept them finally, although I've known some who never do. I've never had any luck with the Bororos or Chavantes, but I'm sure those savages in this settlement don't belong to either of those tribes. I can tell by their footprints."

"More Indians come now," Manolo said. "One very big."

"Action at last," Tom cried. "Jiminy, that Indian waving his arms around must be over six feet tall. What's all that waving about?"

"This may be the first attraction post he's ever seen, and he's probably puzzled by it," Mr. Jason said.

"Say, Uncle," Tom asked, "how can we be sure those Indians are friendly, even if they accept the presents? They may take them and still pepper us with arrows if we get within range."

"Very true, Tom. But most Indians won't accept things from strangers unless they are friendly. And they have different ways of showing they are friendly. You'll see."

For more than half an hour the powwow ashore continued. Suddenly the big Indian stooped and entered the attraction post. A few seconds later he came out with the basket of gifts. Again there was a powwow. And once more the Indians disappeared into the bush.

"Something is bound to happen soon," Mr. Jason said as they sat down to await developments. "If they do something hostile, such as light a bonfire and throw our gifts into it, we'll head for some healthier place. If they hop into their dugouts and come after us the jig is up, of course."

"Here comes the big Indian back," Tom said a few minutes later. "He has three long arrows in his hand, but no bow. What does that mean?"

"Hand me those binoculars for a second, Tom," Mr. Jason said. "I think I know what the Indian is up to, but I want to make sure." Mr. Jason peered through the binoculars intently for a moment without speaking. He watched the Indian break the head off each arrow and bury the broken shaft in the ground. Then the Indian raised both hands over his head.

"Excellent, excellent," Mr. Jason said. "He's telling us we're welcome. It's the usual thing for some tribes in Brazil to show they are friendly by burying headless arrows in the ground and by raising their arms to show they have no hostile weapons. I'm going ashore now. If I'm right, I'll be back for you two."

"Please let me go along, Uncle," Tom said as the missionary brought the skiff alongside.

"Me go, too," Manolo said quietly.

Mr. Jason looked at both and smiled. "I suppose there's no use trying to change your minds. All right, hop into the skiff. I think everything's going to be okay unless this tribe is pulling a sleeper on us."

Tom watched Manolo's smooth strokes with the oars. "Say, Uncle," he began slowly, "if those Indians were hostile would they let us know they were?"

"Chances are they would," Mr. Jason answered. "In the twenty-odd years I've been doing medical and missionary work with the Indians of Brazil, I've always known when they were hostile. Most Indians are children of nature, remember. Don't think they are anything like Manolo, here. They are sly, cunning, very clever in many ways, but simple and natural as babes. It's easy to tell when they fear, like, or hate you."

"Well, Uncle, what would that tribe in there have done if they were unfriendly?"

Mr. Jason glanced at the big Indian whose arms were still raised over his head.

"Any one of a number of things. Some tribes shoot a rain of arrows toward strangers, and that means only one thing, of course. They will refuse gifts. Some burn gifts to make their meaning clearer. Some light fires and throw the likeness of a white man in the flames. In other words, they burn a white man in effigy. Well, we're almost there."

"Do you think these Indians around here have ever seen white men before?"

"That's a hard question to answer. But I do know that few white men—explorers or missionaries—have ever penetrated into this part of the jungle. Most of them who have, never returned to tell the tale. As I said yesterday, I never knew until yesterday that this desolate region was inhabited at all. And, to tell you the truth, I am a bit surprised to find this tribe so friendly."

"Gosh, Uncle. I never saw Indians with such bright red faces and bodies. I thought most of them were copper-colored, like Manolo."

"That bright red isn't their natural color, Tom. Most Brazilian Indians stain their bodies one color or another. Some use a dye made of the waxy paste of a plant called *achiote*. This plant has pink flowers that look something like cherry blossoms and it produces pods that contain red seeds. The Indians crush the pods and smear the stuff all over them."

"That big fellow looks ugly and ferocious, now that we're only a few hundred yards away, doesn't he?" Tom asked. "He doesn't seem to be moving a muscle." Tom glanced at the equipment the missionary had put in the boat. "Why did we bring along the radio and movie projector and salt, Uncle?"

"When I try to teach these heathens I often begin by showing them movies and let them listen to a radio. At times the radio is a very useful gadget, because it mystifies Indians even more than motion pictures do. As a result, they are a lot easier to handle. The first time I showed the Parintin tribe movies they were so scared they all ran off into the woods."

"Does the radio scare them, too, Uncle?"

"Practically always the first few times they hear one."

"Why are we bringing along salt to give them?" Tom asked.

"Ah, Tom, all Indians are crazy about salt. They use it on meat and some of them use salt as an antidote for poison. A paymaster working for a rubber company told me that one night he left a box of salt and eight thousand dollars in his knapsack while he went down to the river to fill his canteen. When he returned the salt was missing, but the money was untouched. That's what Indians think of salt—and money."

"Jeepers, we'll be ashore in a minute. Boy, what a swell fullback that fellow in there would make." Tom lapsed into a reverie. "Wait till I write Mom and tell her I had mango juice, fried bananas and mandioca bread for breakfast, Uncle. Wonder what this tribe around here eats?"

"You never know till you see them. Some eat ants, just as the Shoshone Indians back in Nevada used to consider grasshoppers a delicacy. Most of them eat mandioca prepared in different ways, but fish and game are the preferred food among most of the Indians of Brazil. Well, here we are, lads." Mr. Jason, silent, watched the Indian intently as the skiff neared the shore.

As they approached the Indian, Tom noticed his fierce, arrogant look. His jet black hair was closely cropped. He had a small tuft of feathers in both ears and wore a necklace of seeds of some kind. His loincloth, his only clothes, was made of bark. A bunch of fibers hung down from his girdle in front. Tom watched, fascinated, as the missionary greeted him in various Indian dialects. Finally the Indian grunted something that sounded like a frog croaking. Then he handed each of them one of the headless arrows which he pulled out of the ground.

"He seems to understand the Parintin dialect, although the lingo he speaks is not exactly the same," Mr. Jason said. "I've never run across his language before, but I guess we can get along with my pidgin Indian." Uncle Leo addressed the Indian again. Suddenly his expression brightened.

"*Karana. Nopan karana,*" he said.

"That means welcome. All of us are welcome," Mr. Jason translated.

"*Lana mo Picasto*," the Indian said.

"He says his name is Picasto."

The Indian wheeled and motioned for them to follow.

"He may belong to a branch of the Parintins, but those big toes of his still puzzle me. Let's leave the equipment here for a while until we see what the place looks like. I told him that we are friends of his tribe and that we bring them gifts. He seems to understand."

"Gosh, look at those rippling muscles in his legs and biceps. I certainly would hate to have trouble with him," Tom said as he hurried to keep up with the Indian. Mr. Jason followed him, and Manolo brought up the rear.

"Here's the fork we came to yesterday. He's taking the left-hand path up the hill."

As they threaded their way through the winding path Mr. Jason cautioned Tom to be careful of the six-inch thorns on some of the bushes. A few minutes later they arrived at a clearing rectangular in shape. It was about three hundred yards long and a third as wide. There, waiting to greet them, was an Indian even larger than the first one they had seen.

"He's a good six feet two, at least," Tom whispered. "He looks like the strong man in the circus."

The powerful Indian handed each of them a headless arrow just as Picasto had.

"*Karana,*" he croaked.

"He sounds exactly like a frog," Tom whispered.

The Indian rapped his bare chest with both clenched fists. "*Lana mo Tagana,*" he said. "*Imo gasaka.*"

"He says his name is Tagana and that he is head-man of the tribe," Mr. Jason translated.

"*Picasto mo chulo,*" the Indian said.

"He says Picasto is his brother," Mr. Jason said. He seems to be interested in you, Tom, judging from the way he keeps looking at you." Nobody spoke for a moment as Tagana approached Tom and examined him curiously. He touched his head and elbows, then walked around him three times without saying a word.

"It's my guess," the missionary said, "that he has never seen a white boy before. You haven't been in the tropics long enough to get a good tan, Tom, and he's puzzled by your blond hair and blue eyes."

"I wish he wouldn't keep looking at me as though he were thinking of making me into a stew," Tom said nervously. "He gives me the creeps. These Indians aren't cannibals, are they?"

"They might be, but we won't let them eat us," Mr. Jason said smiling.

"When he finishes inspecting me I'd like to see where he lives," Tom said. "Now he's giving Manolo the once-over."

"He Says His Name Is Tagana."

Tagana looked fixedly at Manolo for a few seconds, then grunted something to Picasto. The latter walked around Manolo muttering and shaking his head. Then both Indians looked at the missionary and Tagana spoke.

When Mr. Jason answered he turned to Tom and Manolo. "Tagana wanted to know what tribe Manolo belongs to, and he can't understand why none of us knows. He wanted to hear you say something in your native language," the missionary said looking at Manolo.

Tagana indicated they were to follow him. He stopped in the center of the clearing and sat down with his legs crossed. Mr. Jason, Tom and Manolo followed suit as Picasto picked up a hollow gourd that was on the ground and began to thump it.

"That gourd is used as a drum," Mr. Jason explained. "There's going to be a show of some kind."

A few minutes later the members of the tribe began trooping into the clearing. They sat around in a semicircle, the men in front of the women.

"Jeepers, they're painted blue," Tom exclaimed. "And look at those feathers on their heads and wrists. These must be their Sunday clothes. Where are Tagana and Picasto going, I wonder."

"They are probably going to switch from red to blue, too," Mr. Jason said. "Listen. The Indians squatting over there are beginning to chant."

A low monotonous chant gradually spread from Indian to Indian. Soon all of the natives, heads bent low and eyes closed, were chanting the mournful strain. "It sounds as though they were singing a funeral dirge," Tom said. "None of those Indians are as big as Tagana or Picasto, are they?"

"No," the missionary replied, "but they are taller and huskier than most Brazilian Indians. And, as often happens, the men rule the roost. Look how browbeaten those squaws look."

"I guess this is their community playground, Uncle," Tom remarked. "Those two-piece outfits the women are wearing seem to be made of tree bark."

"They are," Mr. Jason said. "Here come Tagana and Picasto, all stained blue. Didn't take them very long to change. That headdress Tagana is wearing is made of eagle feathers. The headdresses worn by the other males are made of macaw feathers."

Picasto beat his primitive drum again.

"That's the funniest-looking drumstick I ever saw," Tom remarked. "What's it made of?"

"It's a jaguar bone," the missionary said. "It's just after eleven now. I'd like to know what this ceremony is all about. It could be anything from a birthday party to an execution."

"I'll bet I know," Tom cried excitedly. "That Indian they captured in the pit. They're going to kill him. Look at that fire that Indian is lighting."

CHAPTER FIVE

A STRANGE CEREMONY

The tempo of the mournful chanting suddenly increased as Tagana strode into the center of the clearing and waited with arms folded.

"I counted a hundred and ninety-four men and boys and two hundred and five women," Tom said. "Those women sure look like a bunch of sad sacks. Wonder if any of these Indians ever smile?"

The singing ceased as an Indian maiden entered the clearing. Her eyebrows were shaven, and her face was painted yellow. Tagana sat down and motioned for her to sit beside him.

"That necklace she's wearing is made of jaguar teeth," Mr. Jason said. "This is going to be a wedding ceremony instead of an execution, I think. At least, that's what a necklace of jaguar teeth means among the Mahues tribe. Before an Indian brave can court a maiden he must present her with a necklace made of teeth taken from jaguars he has killed. These Indians aren't Mahues, but they may have the same custom."

"Where did she get the razor to shave her eyebrows with?" Tom asked.

70

"Indians use sharpened bones or bamboo slivers," Mr. Jason replied. "I don't know which method this tribe uses, of course." He paused when an Indian entered carrying a reed basket. He was followed by another Indian who had two straw gloves in his hand. The gloves were adorned with macaw feathers. Picasto beat his drum again. An Indian who appeared to be in his late teens entered and stood before Tagana and the maiden.

"Looks as though he's the groom," the missionary said. "I have an idea what's in that basket, now, but let's wait and see."

Tagana waited until Picasto sat down behind the maiden. Then he rose and barked a command. The Indian with the two gloves of woven straw handed one of them to Tagana. The chief spoke again and the Indian with the reed basket stepped forward. Tagana opened the basket and pulled out something.

"Jumping Jiminy," Tom whispered, "it's an ant. And what a whopper! It's about an inch long."

"Very interesting, very interesting," Mr. Jason murmured half to himself. "That's a tocandeira ant, one of the largest ants in the world. And believe me, Tom, those ants sting like fury."

"Look at what Tagana is doing," Tom said. "He's putting one ant after another into the straw glove."

"The groom-to-be is now going to get the works,"

Mr. Jason told Tom. "This is a trial of endurance and courage. If he flinches when the tocandeiras bite him, there will be no wedding. And it's a rugged ordeal. A tocandeira bit me once three years ago and I felt a sharp pain and had a fever for several hours. I pity that poor young Indian."

"Have you seen this trial of endurance before, Uncle?" Tom asked.

"Not exactly this way," Mr. Jason answered. "The Mahues tribe has a different routine. If a bachelor in that tribe wants to get married he has to prove he can stand bodily pain. He has to pass his arms at least ten times through long stalks of the palmtree which are filled with large, poisonous ants—these tocandeiras. I saw a youngster of fifteen put to the test once. He was led to the chief of the tribe. He had to put on palm gloves full of ants and sing and dance before every hut in the village, accompanied by music. That is, it was supposed to be music. It sounded terrible. He staggered from the pain, but he didn't cry out. When he reached the last hut he was pale and wobbly. His teeth were chattering, his arms were red and swollen from the ant bites. But he managed to hand the gloves back to the chief as the tribal members embraced him. Then he was allowed to jump into a stream where he stayed until night. Those tocandeiras not only bite, but they have a sting much worse than a bee or wasp."

"Tagana put exactly a hundred tocandeiras in that first glove," Tom said in an awed tone as he watched the ceremony. "Now he's filling the other glove."

"These Indians can count up to a hundred at least, then," his uncle replied. "I know tribes who can't count over five. The test is now about to begin."

"He's pulling on the right glove now," Tom said excitedly. "There goes the other one. He's raising the gloves over his head. Wow! I pity him. This is a lot harder than being an eagle scout."

"Look at him," commented the missionary. "Not a sign of pain on his face. That lad has courage to undergo such torture without yelling blue murder."

"I think I'd stay a bachelor if I belonged to this tribe," Tom said, grinning. "No marriage could be worth a million ant bites."

Mr. Jason smiled and patted him on the shoulder. "I'm sure you could pass the test if you wanted, Tom. Your mother told me you played through a whole football game last fall with two broken ribs. You look rugged enough to take care of yourself, even if you're only fifteen."

"Imagine being stung by two hundred ants at once, Uncle. It's a wonder he doesn't faint. But look —he's tottering now—he looks as if he might keel over—" Tom was sickened and impressed by the Indian's unflinching endurance of pain.

"And see how Tagana is crying," Mr. Jason interrupted. "He's crying because he's so pleased that the lad is so brave. Many Indians cry when we would laugh."

Tom watched Tagana pull the gloves off the Indian. He noticed how swollen and inflamed his hands and arms were up to his elbow. The maiden rose and approached Tagana with bowed head. The chief touched her with his right hand, the tortured Indian with his left. "Is that all there is to the ceremony?" he asked. "Are they married now?"

"Righto, Tom," his uncle said as Tagana emptied the tocandeiras into the fire in the clearing.

The silence that had descended during the trial of endurance was broken again by the chanting of the tribal members who were jumping to their feet forming a circle around the fire. The men formed the inner circle, the women a larger circle farther from the fire. Then they began stamping the ground with their feet, moving slowly around the fire as the bride and groom headed for the settlement, which was farther up the hill. Tagana watched the ceremony for a while without speaking. Then he gave an order. Picasto beat his drum and the Indians filed out of the clearing in orderly fashion, the men first. When the last had gone Tagana beckoned for Mr. Jason and his young companions to follow him.

As they headed up trail along a path about four

feet wide, the afternoon rain suddenly descended. But the trees overhead formed a canopy that kept the party from getting wet.

"Where do these Indians get their tocandeiras?" Tom asked as he tramped along between his uncle and Manolo.

"They usually pour some kind of poison over the anthills. It drugs the ants just the way it stupefies fish. Then they collect them and put them in baskets where they revive."

The trail wound down the crest of the hill toward a narrow jungle stream over which there was a rude footbridge made of liana branches.

Mr. Jason stopped on the other side of the stream. Tom followed his gaze. There on a tree beside the stream was a collection of tattered clothes and rags of every description. There was a look of amazement on the missionary's face.

"This," he said slowly, "must be the lost tribe Manolo belongs to."

CHAPTER SIX

EAGLES AND THE CAPTIVE

Tagana led Mr. Jason, Tom and Manolo over the footbridge up a winding trail. Suddenly the Indian chief halted and pulled aside some branches that hid a private entrance to the village.

"Notice the path leading directly to the camp and you'll see why Tagana is taking this route," Uncle Leo whispered. "The other path is covered with sharp bamboo splinters to discourage any enemy from getting within arrow's range of the village. I imagine every avenue of approach is covered with those splinters. And remember that the Indians go barefooted," he continued as they followed Tagana into a circular clearing surrounded by a heavy forest. The trees at the edge of the clearing were cut down to a height of about seven feet. Twenty Indian dwellings or malokas were arranged in circular form at the outer edge of the clearing.

"Those malokas really do look like big beehives, don't they, Uncle?" Tom said. "They're made of palm leaves, aren't they?"

"Yes, Tom. The Indians stick long poles in the ground opposite one another and about thirty feet

76

apart. Then they bring the ends of the poles together at the top and tie them together with vines. They never use nails or mortar, you know, but those thatched malokas are rainproof."

"Are these malokas like the ones you saw in the settlement where you found Manolo?" Tom asked.

"Exactly," the missionary answered as they followed Tagana into a maloka. "The inside is the same, too," he added when they entered. "The same cane partitions dividing the shelter into bedrooms. The same hammocks, the same reception room in the center. This is the lost tribe, all right."

Tagana pointed to two hammocks in one of the bedrooms and grunted something to Mr. Jason. The missionary answered and Tagana, scowling, left with Manolo.

"I told him we would sleep and eat on the *Paloma*, which didn't seem to please him too much. But he insists for some reason that Manolo stay here in camp. I'd like to know just where he's taking Manolo now."

"Jeepers, Uncle, what's the big idea? Manolo won't like staying here, will he? I never saw such a dirty hovel. Look at that junk all over the floor. And, my gosh, what's that huge bowl in the center of the reception room? It's at least ten feet in diameter."

"That's the clay dish the Indians eat from. They probably all eat from it at the same time."

"Well, Uncle, I'm sure glad we don't have to, and it will be awful if Manolo has to. He's used to our ways. Look at the ants and lizards crawling all over it. I wonder who those two women in there on the hammocks are?"

"One is probably Tagana's wife, the other his daughter. Let's take a walk around the village while Tagana is out."

"These Indians must be cannibals," Tom said breathlessly, and pointed toward a wall. "Those skeletons over near the bowl look human, don't they?"

"No, Tom," his uncle explained, "they are monkey skeletons. Let's go."

As they walked around the village they noticed that the area surrounding the malokas was sprinkled with sand. Between the sandy strip and the cut trees was another strip about twenty yards wide covered with bamboo splinters.

"If an enemy managed to get through those splinters he would still leave telltale footprints in the sand," the missionary said. "Some Indians like the roving Magu tribe, can travel surprisingly fast by swinging from tree to tree like monkeys. The men can do it while carrying their weapons and the women while carrying their children. But even the Magus would have a hard time invading this settlement. Can you guess why this camp is built on high land away from rivers and streams?"

"Because there are more mosquitoes near the water?" Tom suggested.

"That's one reason, Tom. Another more important reason they don't camp too near the river is their fear that the sound of the water might prevent their hearing the approach of an enemy. Note, also, that they have cleared the approaches to the camp of all vegetation so no enemy—human or animal—can sneak in undetected. Indians around here have to be especially careful of jaguars. Those bones you see piled in front of some of the malokas are jaguar remains. Tagana's pile is the biggest, so he is probably considered the bravest member of his tribe on that account. At least, that's the way it works with some tribes."

Half of Tom's attention was on his uncle's remarks, and the other half was on his surroundings. Everywhere he looked he saw something new. "Look at those big dugout canoes over there near the secret entrance. There must be about forty of them, and they all seem to be different sizes. I suppose the biggest is Tagana's," he said.

"Probably. It's a good fifty feet long, isn't it? Those canoes are hollowed out from single logs, and it takes several men to handle them," Uncle Leo said as they headed toward an Indian who was starting a fire.

"Those dugouts sure can move along fast, Uncle," Tom said. "We found that out yesterday when they chased us down the river."

They paused to watch the Indian put a stick of hard wood in an arrow shaft and twirl it between the palms of his hand. Then he lit some dry palm shoots which were in a hearth made of wood.

"I never saw a fire made exactly like this," Mr. Jason said with a puzzled expression. "Some Indians make fire by sawing one piece of wood with another and by fanning. I can't quite figure this tribe out. Their big toes are bent like the Motilons. Their marriage ceremony has a lot in common with the Mahues tribe. I know of no tribe that dresses exactly like this one. That girdle of bark is common enough, but that bunch of fibers hanging down from the girdle in front is something new. That seems to be their everyday costume. And you noticed at the marriage ceremony how their bodies are stained blue instead of the usual red. I know of no other tribe that does that."

They stopped to watch an Indian put a tapir in a pit which was lined with red-hot stones. He covered the tapir with earth.

"This tribe cooks just like the Caingang Indians. Notice that they neither skin or cut up animals when they cook them. These Indians really baffle me. Next time we see Tagana I'm going to ask him the name of his tribe."

They passed two husky Indian braves who were tossing a heavy log back and forth for exercise. From time to time they peeked into a maloka as they walked by. Suddenly an Indian emerged from one of the malokas with four large chunks of meat under his arm. The sullen-looking Indian paid no attention to Mr. Jason and Tom as they trailed him. He crossed the sandy area fringing the settlement and dropped the chunks of meat on the ground while he swept a narrow path through the bamboo splinters with a crude broom made of palm leaves. Then he returned for the meat and followed the path he had made. He pulled aside some branches that hid a second secret approach to the camp and descended a gentle slope to a small clearing under the trees. The treetops kept out most of the sunlight, but in the dim light Tom saw an unforgettable picture. Four vicious-looking birds with long hooked beaks and curved claws were tied with liana vines to some poles driven into the ground. The birds were about three feet tall.

"Jumping Jupiter, Uncle Leo," Tom cried. "Those murderous-looking birds look like eagles! And see what they're doing. They're trying to get at the Indian squatting in the center. If one of those vines breaks he's a gone goose."

"Here's another one for your scrapbook, Tom,"

Uncle Leo said, his voice vibrant with excitement. "Those are South American eagles, all right. But it's the first time I've ever seen them used to guard a prisoner. Just look at them tear those chunks of raw meat with their claws. Do you recognize that prisoner?"

"How could I ever forget him, Uncle. The way he's all blacked up. And that grease in his hair. He's the one we saw trapped in the pit."

"Righto," his uncle replied. "He'd probably try to escape while the eagles are busy eating, but if you look over there you can see why he doesn't dare."

Tom wheeled around and looked at the Indian who had taken the meat to the eagles. He was lying on his back holding the bow with the big toe of his right foot. And the arrow in the bow was pointed straight at the captive Indian.

Suddenly Tagana's voice boomed in the silence. He looked fiercer than usual as he stood there a few yards up the path with his arms folded. He had appeared out of nowhere and the sound of his approach was unheard. He whirled around and with an arrogant wave of his right arm indicated that Mr. Jason and Tom were to follow him.

CHAPTER SEVEN

WHITE MAN'S MAGIC

Tom took one last look at the four eagles who were again lunging at the captive. "How does it happen those eagles paid no attention to us?" he asked as he brought up the rear.

"That captive Indian is smeared with monkey fat," his uncle answered. "That's why the eagles are straining at the leash to get at him. With those powerful beaks and claws they'd hack him to pieces in a twinkling."

Tagana led them through the swept path without turning or saying a word. Tom noticed when he glanced back that the Indian who had fed the eagles swept the bamboo splinters back into place and erased the footprints that had been made in the sand. "Maybe," he said, "the captive will try to escape when the birds go to sleep."

"I have a hunch they won't sleep for a while. They seem awfully hungry, and all that meat did was whet their appetite. I also have an idea the prisoner won't be in that strange death cell very long. I'm afraid Tagana will kill him."

Tagana crossed the village to his maloka and sat

down on a jaguar skin in front of it. Mr. Jason and
Tom sat down beside him, and the missionary
waited for him to speak. After they had spoken to
each other for a few minutes the missionary turned
to Tom.

"I've found out that the name of this tribe is
Tapintin. Tagana says he knows nothing about the
Parintins, but I'm sure they must be related in some
way, because he understands many Parintin words."

"Ask him what tribe that captive Indian belongs
to, Uncle."

A fiendish expression appeared on Tagana's face
when Mr. Jason put this question to him. He bared
his teeth for a brief instant then answered with one
word.

"The captive is a member of the Pomora tribe. I
don't know much about them except that they are
head-hunters. Tagana says the Pomoras live deep in
the jungle beyond the Tapajos River and that they
often steal into the Tapintin village at night and attack with poisoned darts. And when he captures
them he puts them to death."

"And what about Manolo? Where is he and when
can we see him?"

"That is what is bothering me," Mr. Jason began
slowly. "Tagana says Manolo is a missing member of
the Tapintin tribe who was lost many years ago. He
says he wants Manolo to remain with the tribe and

marry his daughter, Kalena. This is a very ticklish situation. We've got to be careful not to offend Tagana, because he thinks he is heaping a great honor on Manolo by accepting him as a son-in-law."

"Won't he even let us see Manolo?" Tom asked.

"Not at present. He says Manolo is with his medicine man. I fear poor Manolo will be shocked when he learns of Tagana's intention to keep him here. The Tapintins are so crude and savage Manolo could never be happy with them."

Tagana was watching the missionary closely, as if trying to guess what he was talking about. Suddenly the chief rose and entered his maloka. He squatted at the bowl which was piled up high with cut up fish and meat of some kind. As soon as Tagana took his position at the bowl he was joined by the other males who squatted down around the bowl and began scooping up the food with their fingers. From time to time they groaned and smacked their lips with satisfaction.

"Jeepers, Uncle, they even eat the fish eyes. I never saw such manners." Tom watched them bolt their food. They all stopped eating when Tagana rose. Then the women took their places around the bowl. They ate with the same noisy satisfaction as the men.

After watching them for a few minutes Tom went outside where his uncle was setting up the movie projector and screen. Tagana, who was sitting down on the jaguar robe, was watching the missionary intently. It was now after eight-thirty. The silence of the moonlight night was broken by the sound of the Indian women eating and by an occasional howl of some monkeys in the jungle.

"I told Tagana I'd show him some magic first and then all his tribe could see it," Mr. Jason whispered as Tom drew near. "As far as the Tapintins are concerned, movies are magic. We'll wait a while until the tribe has retired."

The moment the image was flashed on the screen the frightened Tagana jumped to his feet and ran screaming into his maloka.

"I suspected he'd be scared," Mr. Jason said smiling. "Let's go in and see what he's doing."

They found the chief cowering in his hammock muttering to himself. His wife, lying in the hammock above him, and his daughter in the top hammock, looked frightened and bewildered, but they said nothing. Mr. Jason spoke to Tagana, who had first lapsed into a sullen silence, and then begun to rave wildly.

"He is really scared out of his wits," the missionary said. "He thinks the pictures he saw are evil spirits, but I've assured him that nothing will harm him, and he's agreed to see some more."

Tagana, still quaking with fear, followed them

Tagana Screamed in Fright

outside. The missionary showed some movies he himself had taken along the Amazon. One scene showed a dog prancing about in front of an alligator. The chief became excited when he saw it, and he grunted something to the missionary.

"He wants to see that part again," Mr. Jason said, smiling. "He says he wants to see whether the alligator caught the dog."

After seeing the same scene over and over several times Tagana's curiosity was satisfied. When the movie ended he walked up to the screen and inspected it carefully.

"He sure is mystified, all right," Tom grinned. "Shall we let him hear a radio program now?"

"I think we'd better save the radio for later," his uncle said. "It may come in handy in a pinch. We'll row out to the *Paloma* in a little while, but first let's find out something about the religion of the Tapintins. It may have something to do with Tagana's plans about Manolo, you know."

After plying the Tapintin chief with questions for more than half an hour the missionary learned that the tribe worshiped the sun and the moon. "He says the sun sometimes quarrels with the moon and it gets dark," the missionary remarked to Tom. "Right now they are having a fight. He also says they fight because the sun once jilted the moon. The moon wept so bitterly its teardrops formed the Amazon

River."

"I wondered where all that water came from," Tom said jokingly. "What else did he say?"

"He just told me that the sun makes a rainbow when it smiles at the moon. Also, that someday the moon will fall down on the earth and kill all the Pomora Indians." Mr. Jason glanced at the Indian and said, "It's getting past his bedtime. He's beginning to yawn. I'll ask him to guide us back to our skiff."

"I'm getting a bit tired, and I wouldn't mind something to eat, either," Tom said when Tagana disappeared into the maloka. He returned a minute later with the oddest lantern Tom had ever seen. It consisted of a number of fireflies cased in a cage made of bamboo slivers.

"Now I've seen everything," Tom said as he took the movie equipment his uncle handed him. "Imagine using fireflies to light your way."

"That kind of lantern is much safer here in the jungle," his uncle said. "Not as likely to attract any enemy's attention, because the jungle is full of fireflies and nobody would pay any particular attention to them."

"Gosh, Uncle, I hope none of those Pomoras are sneaking around here," Tom whispered as they followed Tagana down the hidden pathway where there were no bamboo splinters. "By the way, did you ask Tagana when he plans to execute his captive?"

Mr. Jason nodded his head. "Yes. He intends to put him to death tomorrow at high noon in the clearing where we saw the marriage ceremony. I told him he should forgive his enemies, but he paid no attention. But I have something up my sleeve that may change his mind," he added as they arrived at the clump of bushes where they had hidden the skiff. Tagana waited until they put the boat into the water before he disappeared into the darkness.

"And what about saving Manolo, Uncle Leo?" Tom asked as he rowed toward the launch. "We can't let him be bitten by all those tocandeiras and spend the rest of his life with savages."

"If our strategy saves the Pomora tomorrow, Tom," the missionary said quietly, "we'll rescue Manolo all right. If it doesn't work, Manolo is doomed."

Tom shivered in the cool night of the Brazilian jungle.

CHAPTER EIGHT

A VOICE SPEAKS

It was a few minutes past ten o'clock when Mr. Jason and Tom dragged the skiff ashore and hid it in a clump of bushes along the river. After making sure they were unobserved hiding the skiff they headed for the clearing which was almost half a mile up from the river.

"I think your idea of keeping a diary while you're in Brazil is fine, Tom," Mr. Jason said as they hurried along. He stopped and pulled aside some tree branches a few feet to the right of the path. "Take a look at that stick insect on this limb," he said. "That's something you've never seen before."

"I don't see anything but a green twig where your machete is pointing, Uncle," Tom said as he moved closer to examine the limb.

When the missionary prodded the object with his machete it moved slightly. "That's a stick insect," he said. "It's enemies have a hard time spotting it because it makes itself look like a green twig which seems to be growing on the tree or plant from which it dangles. This one is only about two inches long, but I've seen stick insects as long as three and a half inches."

"Gosh, Uncle, those stick insects are as clever as chameleons when it comes to camouflage," said Tom.

About fifty yards farther up the trail the missionary pointed with his machete toward a tree that was smaller than most of the others in the area. In it were several black and yellow birds about half as large as crows. They made a racket as if they resented the two visitors. "Here's something else you can note in your diary, Tom," he said. "Those birds up there, which look like orioles, are called caciques down here. In their own way they are just as smart as that stick insect which I showed you. Notice those nests which are more than eighteen inches in diameter. Aren't you surprised to find wild birds building their nests near a trail that is used so much by Indians?"

"But those caciques don't seem afraid of us, Uncle."

"Look at those hornets buzzing around up there and you can see why. See the hornets' nest? The birds figure they are safe while hornets are around to discourage humans from bothering them. Sometimes these caciques build their nests right in the midst of inhabited villages. But only on trees where there is at least one hornet's nest."

"That's good strategy, isn't it?" said Tom as he

ade a notation in his book.

They were close to the clearing when Tom spot-
d an oval-shaped tree that was completely cov-
red by a spider's web, which was at least twenty
et in diameter. On the tree next to it were tiny lit-
e silk monkeys with white markings. Tom made
nother entry in his diary and followed his uncle
to the clearing.

The Tapintins, sullen and silent as before, were
ained a bright blue except for their hair which was
dorned with feather headdresses. They were squat-
ng in a semi-circle as they had at the marriage
eremony, the men in front of the women as usual.

"They're dressed exactly the way they were at the
edding, Uncle," Tom said as he sat down on the
round beside his uncle at the edge of the clearing.
I can understand why a wedding would be a holi-
ay, but why are they wearing all those feathers and
angles when they are to witness an execution?"

"Don't forget they are savages, Tom," his uncle
nswered. "They don't consider murder a crime, nor
o they believe in a trial of any kind. One of my jobs
 to teach them justice and forgiveness. They are
ruel, and like many other tribes down in this part
f the world, they enjoy seeing others tortured and
illed, and the more gruesome the spectacle, the
etter."

The missionary suddenly stopped speaking as two

Tapintin braves dragged the trembling Pomora In
dian into the clearing. The prisoner, his head low
ered, was glancing furtively around like a trappe
animal as if looking for some way of escaping th
doom he knew awaited him. The two Tapintin
dragged him toward a tree at the opposite end o
the clearing from where the tribal members wer
gathered. They used thin strips of liana vines to ti
his arms together behind him. Then they stood hin
in front of the tree and trussed his arms behind
him so tightly he was forced to stoop forward. Ther
was no bravado left in the shifty-eyed Pomora. H
was terrified.

Tagana strutted into the clearing looking like
blue devil. He wore the same costume as his triba
members, including the feather bracelets, but h
fancy headdress was gaudier than those worn b
the other Tapintins. It was made of eagle feather
instead of the macaw feathers, which hung dow
over his back. He walked around in a narrow circl
in the center of the clearing, strutting like a peacoc
Suddenly he barked a command and a Tapintin l
a fire a few yards in front of the Pomora and put
small earthenware pot in it. While it was being hea
ed Tagana picked up a machete and advanced to
ward the Pomora. With it he cut a deep gash in th
trunk of the tree over the Pomora's head as the cap
tive's eyes rolled in their sockets. Tagana returne

to the center of the clearing where he was joined by his brother, Picasto, who struck his gourd three times with the thigh bone of a jaguar. A moment later an Indian carrying a large reed basket entered.

"This is going to be awful, Uncle," Tom said shuddering. "Look at that sap trickling out of the cut in the tree. I'll bet I know what's going to happen. When the Pomora is covered with sap the tocandeiras will pick up the scent and crawl all over him. I just can't bear to even think of it. All that will be left of that poor Indian is bones. Can't we tune in on the radio and stop the execution?"

"Not yet, Tom," the missionary said quietly. "This method of torture I saw used only once before by the Andoke tribe. It was terrible to watch, and at the time I had no radio or movies or victrola with which to stop them. But we won't let Tagana go through with this."

Horrified, Tom watched the dark sap oozing from the cut in the tree and dripping slowly down over the Pomora's head, arms, and chest. Tagana barked another command, and his basket-bearer walked slowly toward the Pomora and stopped. He opened his basket. Tom, as if spellbound, watched the huge black ants crawl out. For a moment they milled around in confusion, as if a signal had been given. Then they headed in a straight line for the sap that had dripped from the Pomora's body to the ground. The Pomora, as if he realized for the first time how he was to die, let out the most piercing scream Tom had ever heard, though none of the tocandeiras had yet crawled up his legs or even touched him. Tom buried his face in his hands.

Tagana gave another order and the Indian who had heated the earthenware pot walked over to the fire and, without changing his expression, picked up the burning hot jar with his bare hand. He carried it in his hand as he walked toward the Pomora and placed it between the captive's bound feet. The victim screamed and kicked it away.

"You see the idea, don't you, Tom?" the missionary asked. "Tagana is showing how much braver the Tapintins are than the Pomoras. And I must admit that the physical courage of the Tapintins matches that of any tribe I know of."

"The Tapintins can take it, all right, Uncle Leo, but they are plenty cruel, too," Tom said.

The missionary glanced toward Tagana and the tribal members who seemed indifferent to the fate of the Pomora. They all had the same bored, sullen expression. "Okay, Tom, here's where we come in. Hand me the portable radio."

The tocandeiras were already crawling up the Pomora's legs when Mr. Jason grimly approached Tagana with the radio tucked under his arm. The tortured victim was shrieking with pain as the ants began to sink their poisonous fangs into his legs. The basket-bearer, who had released several hundred ants, had just sat down with the tribal members when the missionary tuned in on a program. Tagana was advancing toward Mr. Jason with a snarling, fiendish look on his hideously blue face. Suddenly he paused and fell back as a sound came from the radio. In the sudden silence that descended even the tortured Pomora gazed wild-eyed at the mysterious box from which a voice singing a Portuguese song came.

The missionary turned off the radio and spoke gently to Tagana. For a moment the chief looked bewildered and frightened, his eyes opened wide with wonder. Then he waved his arms about and raved as he walked around in a circle. Tom, who had followed his uncle to the center of the clearing, held his breath to see what the outcome would be. Would Tagana punish the missionary for intruding in a tribal ceremony, or would he repent and free the Pomora? "What did you say to him to make him so mad and scared at the same time?" Tom asked his uncle.

"I simply told him the voice in the box came from Bahia, which is hundreds of miles away," Mr. Jason answered. "I told him that he should release the victim and let him go back to his people. He doesn't want to do that, of course, but he fears his gods will punish him. I said nothing about that, but for the present it's just as well to let him think that."

Tagana, as if hypnotized, picked up the machete and walked slowly toward the Pomora, who had begun to shriek again as the ants bit him in dozens of places. The chief paused, glanced backward at the radio, and slashed the vines that bound the victim. As soon as he was free, the Pomora frantically brushed the ants from his body and backed away from Tagana who was pointing with hatred in his eyes toward the trail that led down to the river. The Pomora, glancing wildly about, wheeled and ran whooping down the trail as Tagana savagely trampled on the hundreds of tocandeiras at the foot of the tree. He killed the ones climbing up the tree toward the sap with the broadside of his machete. Then he shouted angrily at the assembled Indians who had lost their bored look the moment the voice came from the mysterious box. They fled in confusion toward the path leading to their village.

All his arrogance gone, Tagana returned to Mr. Jason and Tom, still quaking with fear as he stared fascinated at the radio. Then he numbly headed back toward camp.

"What shall we do about Manolo, Uncle?" Tom asked. "Do you think we can work the radio gag again to save Manolo?"

cade through the overhanging canopy of branches. Tom hastily put his diary in his pocket and peered ┼through the darkness.

"Jumping Jupiter, Uncle Leo, I can't see a thing," he shouted. "Where are you?" There was no reply as Tom squinted into the darkness. The towering trees around him were now dull blurs, inky shapes he could scarcely make out, and the underbrush lining the twisting forest path formed a solid black wall. The cold rain beat down mercilessly, filling the jungle with its deafening roar, as Tom pushed forward noiselessly. He slipped occasionally as he felt his way along the wet tunnel, for the ground had become a slippery carpet. He shouted at the top of his lungs until his voice became hoarse, but still there was no answer.

Thunder echoed mournfully as the tropical storm raged, unbridled in its fury. "Uncle Leo! Uncle Leo!" Tom shrieked, but his voice was drowned out by another peal of thunder. In the momentary flash of lightning that preceded the crash he thought he glimpsed a human form farther down the trail. As he lurched blindly forward he stumbled and fell flat on his face just as a huge tree, struck by a bolt of lightning, toppled with a terrific crash a few yards ahead of him, blocking his advance. He scrambled to his feet as the roll of artillery in the heavens continued unabated. Meanwhile the wind was whis-

tling through the treetops with growing fury, and
the rain beat down in torrents, soaking him to the
skin.

Above the din he could hear a horde of monkeys
howling as they scampered, terrified, from limb to
limb of the trees overhead. It was one of the dreari-
est, most dismal sounds Tom had ever heard, and
as he stood there trying to figure some way of getting past the tree that lay in his path, one of the big
monkeys almost fell on him. For a moment it lay
there on its back, and in a flash of lightning Tom
managed to catch a glimpse of its long whiskers and
shaggy coat of long black hair. Tom backed away
fast as the ugly monkey leaped to its feet and let out
a blood-curdling yell as it crashed into the underbrush.

The piercing screams of what seemed to be hundreds of monkeys were still resounding through the
forest as a flock of loudly chattering parakeets flew
over his head. There were so many of the birds that
the fluttering of their wings could be heard for three
or four minutes as they passed over the trees. The
tropical storm, which had lowered almost without
warning, was raising havoc with the animals in the
jungle. He could see and hear bulky forms he could
not identify bounding across the trail in the midst
of the deafening peals of thunder and blinding
flashes of lightning. He wondered how the moths

d butterflies with their huge, fragile wings could
withstand the fury of such a storm.

Tom stood motionless on the flooded trail as the
wind continued to whistle eerily through the trees.
As desperate as his own plight was at that moment,
he could think only of his uncle and Manolo. There
was one consoling thought. Under the cover of that
storm it would be hard for Tagana and his companion to track down Manolo. There could be no
doubt of it now. Manolo for some reason had escaped from the Tapintin village, and he was being
hunted down by his savage tormentor. Where had
Manolo gone? Where did this trail lead? Would he
ever see his little Indian companion again? The
thought of him being persecuted brought tears to
Tom's eyes. Manolo was proud, and perhaps he preferred to die by himself in the unfriendly jungle to
living with Tagana in the Tapintin village.

Tom felt helpless and confused. He wanted to do
something—he simply had to do something to help
Manolo and Uncle Leo. But what?

He fished his flashlight out of his knapsack and
turned the beam on the immense tree that was
blocking his advance. Should he try to climb
through the tree and search first for his uncle or
wait where he was for the missionary to return? It
suddenly occurred to him that Mr. Jason might be
in danger himself. If not, why didn't he return or

call out to him? He might even have been crush[e]
when the tree toppled over. He might at this ver
moment be lying hurt or unconscious under the tre[e]

Tom whipped out his machete and began to sla[s]
through the branches furiously, calling out to h[is]
uncle as he carved his way. In every flash of ligh[t]
ning he strained his eyes to see if he could discov[er]
any trace of the missionary, and before he hacke[d]
away with his machete, he probed through th[e]
branches with his hands to be sure he didn't strik[e]
the missionary accidentally. He finally cut a pa[s]
sage through the thick boughs and branches an[d]
dropped to the other side. There was no sign of h[is]
uncle, and it was hard in the murky darkness to te[ll]
where the trail led. He felt his way forward cau[s]
tiously, shouting his uncle's name from time to tim[e]
A moment later he was sloshing through the muc[k]
when he sank knee-deep into a depression on th[e]
hunter's trail. As he felt himself going down h[e]
imagined that he was falling into one of the pit[s]
the Tapintins built to ensnare invaders. A gruesom[e]
thought, for if it had been one of those traps, h[e]
might have drowned or have been left to die a slo[w]
death. But it wasn't a pit, and he managed to dra[g]
his foot out. He groped his way forward as fast as h[e]
could. In a sudden flash of lightning he saw tha[t]
the trail forked in two directions. The one leading t[o]
the right narrowed into what looked like a hunter[']

Tom Slashed Through the Branches

trail. Which path should he follow? He decided to take the right for a short distance to see where it led. Then he could return and take the other path which was wider and just as wet.

The howling of the monkeys, which had become fainter as he pressed forward, was now almost drowned out by the heavy downpour that beat down with growing fury. Then once again, farther down the trail, he heard a sound that resembled the grunting of angry hogs. Perhaps they were those dangerous wild boars, which he knew roamed through the jungles of Brazil. Perhaps it would be better to go back, but it was almost impossible to tell from which direction the grunting was coming. He beat his way along, slashing with his machete when the path became too narrow to push through with comfort. Suddenly he breathed a sigh of relief as the storm ceased abruptly—as abruptly as it had begun, and the darkness lifted enough for him to see that he was waist-deep in underbrush that made it hard to go forward.

High up in a tree directly ahead of him he saw dozens of red monkeys, all of whom were grunting like hogs. The monkeys, about the size of an Irish terrier, had long, maroon-colored hair and something that looked like a large lump under their jaws. Tom was about to push forward when something fell from the tree where the monkeys were. He

picked up a hard round shell about six inches in diameter. It was a cluster of Brazil nuts. "Boy, oh
boy," he murmured aloud, "if that had conked me
it would have been curtains." It was hard to tell
whether the nut had fallen accidentally or had been
dropped by the leering monkeys.

Tom felt half suffocated as he slogged forward in
the muck. The hot late afternoon sun beat down on
the rain-soaked jungle now, making it steaming and
hazy. But he could see better through the haze than
he could during the storm. He glanced at his watch.
Twenty past three. He would continue for a while
and then return to the fork if he could find no trace
of his uncle or Manolo. They might have taken the
left turn at the fork. The odor of rotting vegetation
was more stifling than ever. He paused again at the
sound of a loud squawking and glanced up at a tree.
He saw a tremendous parrot, by far the largest he
had ever seen. It was a bright green with yellow-
tipped tail and wings. And its tail appeared to be at
least a yard long as it fluttered from the towering
tree to another even higher one near-by.

Ten minutes later Tom heard more monkeys
howling. He stole forward in the direction of the
sound. Through the dense foliage he saw a number
of monkeys of medium size on the ground. On the
very top of the tree a single monkey was chattering
away. The howling of the monkeys on the ground

ceased as soon as the lone monkey began chattering, and when he ceased they applauded with loud groans and screeches. Tom remembered hearing his uncle speak of the preacher monkeys of the Brazilian jungle. And here they were! He gazed at them, fascinated.

Suddenly one of the monkeys saw Tom, and quick as a flash he relayed the information to his companions who immediately disappeared into the twilight of the jungle. Tom raced after them to see where they went, but they vanished as their howling faded. Tom was about to return to the hunter's trail when he saw, half hidden behind the trees, something that made him think he was dreaming. There, in the heart of the jungle, was a tall, round bamboo building.

CHAPTER TEN

THE BAMBOO TOWER

As he approached the bamboo building Tom could see that it resembled the silos he had often seen on farms in Massachusetts. As he drew within a few yards of it he crouched behind a tree for a few minutes to be sure nobody was near. Then he stole up to it and inspected it from all sides.

It had no windows he could see, and seemed to have no doors. He walked around it several times looking for an entrance of some kind. But it was no use. His wrist watch told him it was almost four-thirty. Perhaps it would be wiser to go back to the village to see whether his uncle had returned and to learn what had happened to Manolo. Suddenly he stiffened and listened intently. He heard footsteps approaching.

Tom ducked quickly behind a tree and waited with bated breath. His imagination began to play tricks on him. It might be a head-hunter—perhaps another Pomora snooping around. It might be a cannibal or a gorilla or an ape. It might even be some hermit who lived in the mysterious green tower—certainly a strange structure to be found so far from civilization. Or it could be Manolo or Uncle Leo.

Now that Tom could hear the footsteps more distinctly, he thought they sounded as though they were made by someone wearing shoes. Tom could hear the steps begin to fade as if the human or animal making them had continued past the spot where he had broken through the brush. As silently as he could, he headed back toward the hunter's trail. When he reached it he peered through the underbrush on the edge of the trail. He saw a familiar figure about thirty yards ahead of him.

"Uncle Leo!" he shouted. "Wow! Am I glad to see you! I fell behind you during the storm, I guess. And did you ever see such a terrible rain?"

"Tom, my boy!" the missionary said in a relieved tone. "You certainly startled me when you popped out of nowhere. I was so afraid you were lost, and I've been searching for you all over the place."

"You must have taken the left-hand trail at the fork, Uncle," Tom said.

"I did," Mr. Jason answered. "I just took it for granted that you were following me, and when it finally dawned on me that you weren't, I backtracked, and when I returned to the fork, I took the other path."

"Gee, Uncle it really was scary in the dark with all that thunder and lightning and all those monkeys making such a terrific racket. By the way, what kind of monkeys make a sound that is something like the grunting of hogs?"

"I know the kind you mean," his uncle said. "Some are black, others red. They have a thin bone in their windpipe that causes them to make that peculiar sound. Under their jaws they have a large swelling, did you notice?"

"I sure did. And what about Manolo? Any sign of him?" Mr. Jason's relieved expression changed to one of worry and anxiety. "Not a sign of the boy. And Tagana and the other Indians disappeared into the blackness. I'd like to know why Manolo ran away. He wasn't trying to get away from us, of course, but he must have had a strong motive for escaping."

"Poor Manolo," Tom said with a sigh. "He must be starved unless he ate some of that terrible Indian chow. And I hope he didn't get lost in this wilderness."

"I'm not too worried about that. Manolo could live indefinitely in the jungle. He could find his way back no matter where he went merely by breaking twigs as he went along, as I've learned to do from the Brazilian Indians. And don't worry about Manolo going hungry. He could live on the berries, fruits and nuts he knows where to find. But he's been frightened somehow, and it's our job to find him."

"I hope Tagana doesn't find him before we do," Tom said grimly. "He may already have found him for all we know."

"That is exactly what is worrying me, Tom," the missionary said as they sat down at the edge of the path to rest for a moment. "I fear Tagana was able to follow his tracks until the storm broke and it got too dark to spot the tracks. But he probably picked up the trail again when the storm lifted. Most of these jungle-wise Indians can tell even by trampled leaves and bruised vegetation where a trail leads. Some of their powers are uncanny. For example, I've seen Brazilian Indians talk to one another across wide streams when I could hardly hear the ones beside me talking. Their sense of hearing and sight is simply amazing. And did you ever hear of their jungle telephones?"

"No! Tell me about it while we're resting. And then I've got something that will interest you. I'm tired out with all this tramping through the woods."

"I wish you'd stop looking so mysterious, Tom," Mr. Jason said. "But I guess I'll have to be patient and wait to see what you have to show me. Oh, yes, about those jungle phones. It's quite similar to the system used by the African bushmen. There are certain trees down around here whose shell is almost as hard as metal. The Indians hollow out the insides of

them with fire, so that when they are struck with a
hard object a sound is made that carries a surprising
distance. There are other such trees at certain spots
known to a tribe. Messages can be picked up by
placing the ear against these hollow trees, and in
this manner messages can be relayed fast through
the jungle. Of course many tribes use smoke signals,
too."

"Pretty slick system," Tom said. "And no phone
bills, either. And now for that surprise I promised
you."

"Fine, Tom," Mr. Jason said as he rose and
yawned wearily. "Then we'd better head back toward camp and see what's up. Why, where are you
going?"

"I just stumbled onto this thing by mistake when
I broke through here to see what was going on,
Uncle," Tom said as he led the way. "I saw the
strangest thing back in there. It is a big bamboo
building that seems to be empty, as far as I could
tell. I was giving it the once-over when I heard your
footsteps."

"I know you aren't joking, Tom, but your story
certainly sounds fantastic. Surely there are no Indians living around here so close to the Tapintins.
I wonder if they know about this building you are
talking about."

"It doesn't have any doors or windows." Tom saw

the look of surprise on his uncle's face when he
paused for a moment and turned around. Then he
pushed toward the building. "You won't believe it
until you see it, Uncle. It's just a few yards farther
in this underbrush."

"It could be a storehouse of some kind," the missionary mused, "or a jail or a temple. But why would
any of those things be tucked away in such a remote
spot? It's about a mile and a half from here to the
village, wouldn't you say?"

"Just about, Uncle. We're almost there. It's just
beyond that big Brazil-nut tree."

A few minutes later they could see the tower in
the fading afternoon sunlight. Mr. Jason looked at it
for more than a minute without speaking. He shook
his head as if he couldn't believe what he saw.

"It beats me, Tom. It almost looks as though it
grew there, doesn't it?" Suddenly he pulled Tom by
the arm. "Watch out for that bush just ahead of you,
Tom. You'd better slip on your leather gloves. That's
pringamora, and it's twice as bad as poison ivy. If
you touched it with your bare skin it would cause a
severe inflammation."

"Maybe whoever built this mysterious bamboo
tower put it here on purpose, Uncle," Tom said, "so
the pringamora would poison anyone who got too
close to it. Just the way the caciques use hornets for
watchdogs, right?" Tom seemed lost in thought for

a moment as they stood there and surveyed the situation. "Gosh, Uncle, I almost ran right into that
pringamora a while ago when I came in here."

"Let's sit down here again and get our wind,
Tom," the missionary said. "This might be a good
time for me to warn you about jungle growths. You
see, I expect to see a good deal of you in the future,
and I want you to know all about what you may run
up against."

"You mean, Uncle Leo, that you're going to invite me to spend another summer with you?" Tom's
voice cracked with excitement.

Mr. Jason looked at his nephew affectionately.
"You can come back next summer if you think you
can stand the mosquitoes and ants and jaguars."

"Boy, oh boy, Uncle," Tom answered happily,
"thanks a million. I accept with pleasure. That re-
minds me, I haven't even seen an ocelot yet, except
for Ozzy. But what about those poisonous plants?"
he said as he pulled on his leather gloves.

"Well, Tom," the missionary began as he settled
comfortably on the damp ground, "there are plants
down here that catch insects and—"

"Like the Venus's-flytrap?" Tom asked.

"Righto. Only some of the big plants down here
are capable of catching animals as well as insects.
I've never run across any of them, but there may
even be some capable of trapping human beings as

there are in Madagascar. Ever hear of the man-eating tree?"

"Jeepers, what a thought!" Tom exclaimed. "Tell me about them. I think I'll stick to the beaten path after this while I'm in the jungle."

"Yes," the missionary continued, "man-eating plants. It's a tree that grows very high. It has leaves as wide as ten or twelve feet. These leaves have thorns like claws, and when a man or an animal gets too near them the leaves close in on them and stay closed for three or four days until the flesh has been digested. Then the leaves open and the bones drop out. I might add that such trees, as well as the Venus's-flytrap, can suffer from indigestion."

"Boy, I hope we never run into any of those trees. Well, Uncle Leo, what do you think of the building?"

"Let's inspect it, Tom. But remember what I said about that poisonous plant. There may be others near here. They walked around the building cautiously, pausing from time to time to see if they could be observed. They listened intently, but not a sound came from the tomblike structure. "It may be some sort of a burial place, Tom," Mr. Jason said. "Otherwise I can't understand why it's all sealed up. Seems to be about twenty-five feet in diameter, doesn't it?"

"Yes, Uncle Leo," Tom answered. "But, gosh,

"It beats me," the missionary answered, shaking his head. "But we'll soon see. Lucky we have our mosquito nets on our helmets. Those pests are pretty thick around here."

The Tapintin finished whatever he was doing. Now and then some monkeys broke the stillness, and the muffled sounds of animals moving about in the jungle could be heard. The area was buzzing with insects and occasionally the croaking of frogs or the piping of other creatures could be heard.

"I see what he's up to," Tom said breathlessly. "The entrance is underground, and it's camouflaged with leaves."

"That's what I just was thinking. But what about those dead monkeys? It couldn't be a burial place for monkeys, of course. Any the Tapintins can't eat they probably throw to the buzzards. And I'm pretty sure now that it isn't a temple. The Tapintins are moon and sun worshipers, and I don't see any connection between that and dead monkeys."

Suddenly the Indian descended, stooping, into the ground and disappeared from view. The muffled sound of something opening could be heard. Then a dull thud as it shut.

"Quarter past six," Mr. Jason whispered. "I hope he doesn't stay in there long. I'm getting hungry, aren't you?"

"I could eat one of those giant parrots I saw

there," Tom said and grinned.

"Here, nibble on this piece of sugar cane, Tom," his uncle whispered. "Parrots are tough eating. Almost as bad as macaw. But if we are hard up we'll catch a parrot and roast it over the fire. This sugar cane will give you quick energy," he added as he bit a piece himself.

"Here he comes," Tom whispered excitedly. The Tapintin came out of the pit, replaced the camouflage and left without the monkeys. Not until several minutes after his footsteps died away did the missionary straighten up.

"Okay, Tom, let's go," he directed. "We've got to untangle this mystery. I'm glad I have a flashlight in my kit. It's going to be pretty dark. And it must be damp and smelly if they keep dead monkeys in there."

They removed the covering hiding the secret entrance. Mr. Jason carefully slid down the slanting clay wall and found himself in a dark, square pit about ten feet deep and eight feet square on each side. In the pitch darkness he probed about, feeling the wall until he located what seemed to be a door. He discovered it was locked when he tried to push it in.

"Okay, Tom, come on down. The wall slants enough so we can get in or out without too much trouble. Maybe both of us can heave in this bamboo door."

Mr. Jason lit up the pit with his flashlight. The walls were lined with bamboo shoots interwoven with liana vines like the building itself.

"Up there on the right, Uncle," Tom said. "That knotted vine must be what's preventing us from shoving in the door."

"Nice work, Tom," his uncle said as he untied the knot. He put the vine strip, about fifteen inches long, in his pocket. "We want to be sure to leave everything just the way we found it so nobody will know we've been here," he said.

They pushed in the door and listened. "I can't hear a thing," Tom whispered.

"Neither can I," the missionary said. He turned the light up the narrow passageway which led to a trap door about fifteen feet above. Tom crept after him up the passageway, which was made of some kind of reeds. It was hard to tell what kind, even with the flashlight.

"I'll push up this trap door," Mr. Jason whispered. "Pretty fancy architecture for savages, isn't it?"

Tom pushed back his mosquito net and mopped his brow with a bandana handkerchief. "It sure is hot in here, Uncle. And the suspense is awful. Maybe this shack is full of gold like one of the temples of the Incas."

"But gold wouldn't explain the monkeys. Be ready

to make a quick exit, Tom. I'm going to raise the circular door now."

At first they could hear nothing when the missionary did this. Then, as they strained their ears to listen, they picked up a sound of something scratching on a hard surface. Mr. Jason let the trap door fall gently.

"What do you make of it, Tom? The walls look black. I could hear a scratching sound, but I have no idea what is making it."

"Neither do I, Uncle. Let's take another peek."

The missionary cautiously pushed up the trap door. He felt the lower part of the wall with his knuckles. It was cold and slimy and hard. He jabbed his hunting knife into the wall. There was a metallic click.

"It sounds as though the inside of the tower were lined with steel," Tom said.

"I think it's wood of some kind. The Tapintins never heard of steel walls. It is probably ironwood which, when dry, is so hard the sharpest ordinary saw can't cut it. Think how clever these Indians were to fit those beams in so snugly. Because that's just what they did." As he spoke he felt the bottom of the wall again with the backs of his fingers. Suddenly he withdrew his hand and let the trap door fall with a bang.

"Tom, it's unbelievable. There are ants in there,

if I know my stings. One of them just sank his tweezers into my hand. I'd better put some ointment on the bite right away to keep from getting an infection."

"Jumping Jupiter, Uncle Leo! What a silly place to find ants. But I suppose they get into everything."

"Those ants didn't find their way in there, Tom," the missionary said, sitting down on the passageway for a moment to put on the ointment. "And they can't get out of their prison, either. They are tocandeiras, and they were put in there."

"So that's where the Tapintins get their tocandeiras, Uncle! I wonder how many there are. And those dead monkeys. I get it now. That was food for the tocandeiras."

"Right, Tom," said Mr. Jason as he rose and turned the beam of light on the trap door again. "Take a quick look when I open this door. I have a hunch the place is swarming with them." Tom followed the beam of light as it moved slowly around the wall and the ceiling. There were ants everywhere. Huge black tocandeiras. Thousands of them were crawling over the three monkeys. Almost every square inch of the interior of the building was covered with them.

"There are millions," Mr. Jason said in a tone of awe. "Millions of them. Perhaps billions. And we want no part of them. Let's get out of here fast."

Tom had never seen his uncle so excited before.

It was dark when they emerged from the pit and replaced the covering. "It's going to be ticklish getting out of here without a flashlight, Tom. But it would be dangerous to use the flashlight. It might attract jaguars or something worse."

"I have an idea, Uncle Leo," Tom said. "I'll catch some fireflies. There are enough of them zooming around. And we'll make our own lantern. If the Tapintins can do it, so can we."

The missionary looked admiringly at his nephew. "Tom, I must write your mother about what a clever youngster you are. Only fifteen and you have outsmarted me a dozen times already in less than two weeks. We'll need about twenty or twenty-five of them. But let's see, we need something to put them in."

"What about my mosquito net?" Tom asked.

"Excellent, excellent," Mr. Jason smiled. "But let's use mine instead of yours. I've been roaming around in the jungle so many years my skin is like leather."

"I'm glad these fireflies are so sluggish," Tom said as he caught one after another and wrapped them in the mosquito net. "I have almost thirty of them."

"Good. Let me take the lantern, Tom. I'll lead the way. This time keep as close to me as you can. I wouldn't want you to get lost at night in this wild place. The fire the Tapintins keep burning in the village at night might attract jaguars, and it's just as well that we don't run into them. They are a bit more ferocious than tigers or lions, you know."

"You know, Uncle Leo," Tom said as he followed him, "I meant to ask you why the Tapintins keep a fire going at night. I should think it would attract so many jaguars and other animals it would be awfully dangerous."

"True, Tom. But Tagana figures human enemies are more dangerous than animals, and he probably reasons that it's harder for them to approach the malokas at night when the village is lit up by the fire."

It was slippery going in the dark mist, for the moon was shut out on every side by the overhanging trees. The lantern of fireflies gave a ghostly green light. The missionary paused from time to time when Tom lost his footing, and once he tripped and fell himself.

"This is really eerie, Uncle, but I love it," Tom said. "Gosh, it must be getting late. I think I could sleep standing up."

"I think we'd better stay in the village with the Tapintins tonight, Tom," his uncle said. "It's quite a trip to the *Paloma*, and besides, I'm anxious to be around in case Manolo is in any danger. Be sure to remind me to get the radio. I have a feeling we are going to need it very shortly."

A few minutes later they reached the clearing

where the four eagles were kept. The missionary lifted the crude lantern to see whether the birds were sleeping. He gasped and fell back.

"Heaven protect us, Tom," he said. "It's Manolo."

Tom raced to his uncle's side.

"Oh, Uncle Leo," he groaned, "this is horrible. The eagles are guarding Manolo. Tagana must be planning to kill him tomorrow."

CHAPTER TWELVE

THE MISSING RADIO

On they came in perfect military formation, a column of gigantic black ants. There was a battalion of warrior ants in front, followed by an orderly procession of worker ants, which were twice as small as the inch-long warriors. The workers were carrying tiny bits of grass, and some carried the bodies of their dead companions. Others had spiders, crickets, roaches and beetles in their pincer-like jaws. As they advanced in a column ten yards wide and two miles long the animals of the jungle were frantically hurrying out of the path of their invasion. Huge snakes slithered before them, and jaguars, elephants and lions rushed to get out of their way.

From the swaying limb of a tree three hundred feet tall and fifty feet in circumference Tom watched, frozen with horror, as the black army of tocandeiras slowly advanced toward the tree in which he had sought shelter. He felt safe as he looked slowly down along the dark ribbon that extended as far as he could see in the bright daylight of the green jungle. On and on they came, in strict military formation, their tiny black eyes glinting savagely in the sunlight.

They closed the gap slowly, relentlessly, but Tom felt sure that he was safe from harm, so high was he in the tree. They were only ten yards away now, and now only five. In just a few seconds he would be able to see them pass the tree. He wondered where they were heading.

Tom's breath was coming in short gasps as he saw the first battalion of warrior ants reach the bottom of the tree. Then, to his horror, the whole column stopped, as if the leader or leaders had given a command. They stood still for five or ten seconds. Then the advance columns wheeled toward the base of the tree. They were beginning to crawl slowly up the bark toward him on every side. It was he they were after. Instead of avoiding their clutches, he was now hopelessly trapped!

Tom's terrified shriek echoed hollowly as he called out to his uncle for help. But Mr. Jason was nowhere to be seen. There was nobody around who could save him now, nowhere he could turn. He scrambled out to the end of the thick limb and hung on by his hands. He tried to shout, but no sounds came from his lips. He hung on for what seemed hours. His arms began to ache, and he felt too exhausted even to move his lips any longer.

The only sound he could hear was the scratching noise made by the tocandeiras as they crawled closer and closer to him. What had happened to all the birds of the forest? Why couldn't he hear the buzzing of insects and the howling of monkeys? Why had such a tomblike silence suddenly descended on the noisy jungle? Was it because every living creature had fled in the fear of being destroyed by the murderous ants?

His left hand slipped as he turned to look down at the approaching tocandeiras, and for a moment he dangled there high in the air, holding on by his right hand. He tried to raise his left arm to regain his grip, but he had no strength left for that. He was doomed. His right arm was getting weaker and weaker, and it was getting harder and harder for him to catch his breath. And, meanwhile, the ants were drawing closer on every side. There was no use trying to shinny down the tree now. He should have thought of that before. He should never have allowed himself to become trapped.

The first ants were swarming over the thick bough which he was grasping with one hand. They were inches now from his fingers. As he felt the first stings he looked down at the ground that seemed so far below him. Another sting, and now another. He felt his eyes closing, and then he felt himself let go. He was drifting, drifting, falling faster and faster, the tocandeiras raining down on him as he plummeted through space. Down and down he went for what seemed long minutes, until suddenly the ground rose up toward him. It was covered with ants, big black ants, tocandeiras!

"Uncle Leo! Uncle Leo!" he shouted as he opened his eyes.

He had the sensation of a blinding fla of light bursting before his eyes. It was the dazzli morning light of the tropics. The clear blue sl above seemed somehow unreal, and the lofty greei all around seemed strange. He blinked as a rair cloud of hummingbirds flew overhead and wer lost from view over the treetops. The sun made the dewdrops sparkle on the branches of the trees, and the early morning breeze rustled through the branches. The air was filled with the chirping of birds and the whirring of wings. Tom sat up and shook the drowsiness from his head.

"What in the world have you been shouting about in your sleep, Tom?" Tom grinned with embarrassment as he looked up at his uncle, who was standing before him with his hands on his hips. He rose dizzily to his feet and rubbed his eyes.

"Gosh, what an awful nightmare I had, Uncle Leo," he said. "I dreamed I was way up in a tree. Just as an army of tocandeiras were about to attack me I fell out of the tree and landed on a few million more. It was all so real. What time is it, Uncle?" he asked as he stretched his arms out to full length.

"It's a few minutes after dawn. You should have seen the way you were turning and tossing in your sleep, Tom. I figured you were having a bad dream."

Tom felt a sense of well-being as he drank in the cool morning air. Once more the jungle seemed friendly. "You have no idea how relieved I feel to know it was only a dream, Uncle Leo," he said grinning. He saw that he had been sleeping on the ground under a tree near the clearing where the four eagles reigned. Suddenly he remembered what had happened the night before. "Manolo! How is he, Uncle? Is he safe? Those eagles haven't broken loose."

"He's all right for the moment, Tom," his uncle said gravely. "He's taking it like the good soldier he is. I've been awake most of the night to see that everything was all right. The eagles finally went to sleep, and then I did. But we have to get him out of this jam, and it won't be easy. Tagana is up to no good."

"Can we talk to Manolo now?"

"Yes, let's see how he is. He's only a few yards away, you know."

Manolo was sitting quietly in the clearing, still hemmed in by the eagles. He smiled wanly at his friends and waved a greeting without speaking. He looked resigned, but unafraid.

"Doggone, Manolo, how we've missed you," Tom

said with tears in his eyes. "And don't worry," he added firmly. "We'll get you out of this if it's the last thing we ever do."

"Manolo says Tagana is still determined to make him marry his daughter," Mr. Jason said as he and Tom stood there out of range of the eagles.

"Never marry Tapintin maiden," Manolo said quietly. "Die first."

"You can say that again, Manolo," the missionary said. "Tell Tom about your escape."

"Tagana take me to maloka of medicine man. He talk like crazy man and I do not understand any word he say. Then, when dark comes, he make me drink bitter herb. I sink into long sleep. When I wake maloka is empty. Village is empty. Nobody there. I know when I hear drums that Tapintins are in clearing on other side. I know there is secret way from camp up there." Manolo waved toward the village. "So I quickly leave. I feel sleepy still. My plan is to hide until chance comes to go down to river and swim to *Paloma* to find my friends. But Tagana and other Tapintin find me when I sleep high in tree."

"I think the best plan is to talk to Tagana, lads," Mr. Jason said. "Tom, you and I will go up there and get the radio. I was saving it for something like this. And we had better go soon before Tagana gets any more ideas."

The Eagles Stood Guard Over Manolo

"Hide quick," Manolo whispered suddenly. "Someone come down trail."

Mr. Jason and Tom ducked out of sight just in the nick of time. Through the underbrush they saw a Tapintin approaching. He was carrying a reed basket. He walked past Manolo staring straight ahead as if he didn't see him.

"He's going down to the bamboo tower for some tocandeiras, Uncle," Tom whispered. "And it's either for Manolo's trial of endurance or—"

The missionary waited until the Tapintin disappeared down the trail. Then he motioned for Tom to follow him as he stole back toward Manolo. "I forgot to ask you, Manolo," he said. "Did Tagana tell you anything about having to kill jaguars so you could make Kalena a necklace of teeth?" he asked.

Manolo shook his head without speaking. Mr. Jason turned to Tom. "As we've learned by this time, Tagana's mind is hard to read, Tom. It's strange that he would change a tribal custom for a stranger like Manolo."

"I hate to say it, Uncle Leo," Tom whispered so Manolo couldn't hear him, "but maybe he hasn't changed any tribal customs. Maybe that Tapintin is getting tocandeiras for an execution rather than for a marriage ceremony."

"I know, Tom." The missionary looked grim. "That would account for the fact that Manolo is being guarded by the eagles, too. On the other hand, Manolo is so attractive, Tagana may be willing to change a rule or two. And because Manolo escaped once, he may be keeping him here simply as a safeguard. But as far as Manolo and we are concerned, it doesn't matter which Tagana has in mind. If he had to stay here it would be a living death anyway. And we've got to prevent that." Mr. Jason picked up his kit as he spoke. "Okay, Tom, let's go. And munch on this piece of sugar cane until we get something better to eat."

The village was quiet when they entered. "They may be having breakfast," Mr. Jason said as they walked past the bamboo splinters and the sand. "They retire soon after sunset and wake around four or four-thirty in the morning if they are like most Brazilian Indians I know. They chatter in their hammocks for a while and then go down to the river for a dip around five a.m. I know the Tapintins do this, because Tagana told me so. Let's go into Tagana's maloka and get the radio. That's the thing we need most now. We can always eat, can't we?" he smiled.

The members of Tagana's household, squatting around the family bowl, were making the usual noisy sounds as they gulped down the warmed-over remains of the previous night's meal which was heaped in the huge container. None, including Tagana, looked up when they entered.

"Imagine eating warmed-over fish and monkey meat for breakfast," Tom said disgustedly as they walked by the Indians.

"They eat only twice a day," Mr. Jason remarked as they walked toward the hammock where Tom had put the radio the afternoon before. "But they eat enough to last them for a while."

"Why, Uncle, the radio isn't where I left it," Tom exclaimed as he searched through the hammocks in Tagana's cabin. "I left it right here in Tagana's hammock."

"Hmmm. I don't like it, I don't like it," his uncle muttered as if he were talking to himself. "I would have sworn none of the Tapintins would have dared touch it. But as I said, they are a hard tribe to figure out."

"And it's the only portable radio we have with us," Tom said gloomily. "It looks as though we're stumped unless we find it."

CHAPTER THIRTEEN

AN EARLY CELEBRATION

Mr. Jason and Tom sat down on the jaguar robe and waited until Tagana finished his breakfast. Neither spoke, and it was clear that both were thinking hard.

"Here it is already July," Tom sighed. "This summer is going too fast. By the way, what's the date exactly?"

"Let's see," his uncle answered. "I have to think, it's so easy to lose track of the time down here. It must be the second, I guess." He turned as Tagana came out of the maloka and sat down beside them. After greeting him cordially, the missionary told him bluntly he wanted the radio immediately. For a moment a hunted look crept into Tagana's eyes as if the memory of the mysterious box still haunted him. Then he ranted and raved in his usual manner. Mr. Jason interrupted and told him the radio would not ever speak again unless someone knew how to work it. Tagana spoke again, this time less excitedly, and pointed toward the sun as he did so. Then he stalked off to Picasto's maloka.

"It looks bad, Tom," the missionary said as he sat

141

down again on the jaguar skin. "Tagana is talking a lot of nonsense, but there is nothing we can do about it, it seems. He said something about his medicine man hiding the speaking box last night while the sun and moon were quarreling. He said he was afraid the moon might fall on the Tapintins instead of on the Pomoras if the sun and moon find out he is listening to strange gods."

"What about the movies, Uncle?" Tom asked. "Couldn't we use them to make Tagana see reason?"

"Well, I am not too sure, now. They wouldn't be nearly so effective, of course, in the daylight, and anyway I doubt whether Tagana fears them as much as he did the radio. And he seems less afraid of the radio now. I wish I had talking pictures, but unfortunately these silent films are the only ones I have with me."

"Look, Uncle. There goes Picasto to the center of the village. Something is up."

"Picasto is probably sounding the first signal for a ceremony. And we still don't know what the ceremony will be. Tagana refused to tell me."

"Gee, Uncle," Tom said dropping down beside him, "we haven't much time to do anything. It's almost seven-thirty already."

Mr. Jason thought hard. "We have about four hours, haven't we? The ceremony, no matter what kind it is, always starts at high noon. Tagana explained the reason for that. It is then, he says, that the smile of the sun is brightest."

"Say, Uncle," Tom said as if he were thinking to himself. "It often rains in the early afternoon, and sometimes around noon. What would happen if it did today? Or suppose it just got cloudy at noontime?"

"I imagine that in that case Tagana would postpone the ceremony until the smile of the sun returned another day at noon. But if that happened today it would be almost miraculous. It hasn't rained until early afternoon, at least, since we've been in the vicinity of the Tapajos River, so I don't think we can count on that."

"Gosh, Uncle, I wish we could have a brain storm. Two of us against a whole tribe. And those weapons stacked over there between the malokas of Tagana and Picasto look menacing, too, don't they?"

"They certainly do. And remember, Tom, as a missionary and physician I am not allowed to use weapons against the Indians of Brazil, even to save my own life. I am required to use peaceful measures."

"Well, Uncle," Tom said seriously, "I didn't have any idea in mind of using weapons against the Tapintins. But I noticed that they don't take their weapons along when they go down to the clearing for their ceremonies. Couldn't we hide them while they are busy down there?"

"I suppose we could, but when Tagana found out he probably would never forgive us. And don't forget that I still have hopes of making Christians out of these pagan Indians. No, Tom, our only real weapon is persuasion of some kind, and that doesn't seem to be working. If we ran for it after getting Tagana mad in some way, the Tapintins would overtake us before we could reach the river. You could probably outrun them on a straightaway, or at least some of them, but remember that it's a narrow winding trail leading down to the river, and the Tapintins are far more used to it than we are."

Tom walked over to examine the bows and arrows. He picked up one of the arrows and turned toward his uncle. "Gosh, this thing is heavy. And look at those eight-foot bows."

"You'd better put that arrow down, Tom," his uncle warned him, "before any of the Tapintins notice you. They might get suspicious."

Tom sat down again beside his uncle. "I don't see how those heavy arrows could ever hit the mark, Uncle."

"Well, my boy," the missionary explained, "as a matter of fact when Indians shoot them distances of more than twenty or thirty yards they have to discharge them at an elevation so they describe an arc.

And it's really amazing how accurately they can figure out the arc. They seldom miss, even at distances up to a hundred or a hundred and fifty yards. I've seen Brazilian Indians aim at buzzards on the beach and hit the exact spot the birds left. And I've seen them hit small birds and anteaters and honey bears at seventy or eighty yards."

"Say, Uncle, couldn't we threaten Tagana without shooting him? What would happen if we aimed a couple of arrows at him when he returns and threatened to shoot him if he doesn't release Manolo?" Tom reached for a bow and stroked it as he talked. If only he could show this bow to his scout troop back home.

"Two armed men against a whole tribe wouldn't work, I'm afraid, Tom, even though the tribe was unarmed. But those bows and arrows aren't the only weapons the Tapintins have. They have blowguns, too. And they can heave stones more accurately than any big league pitcher or football player can throw a baseball or a football. Some Indian tribes keep chickens, for example, and when they want one for supper they kill them with a single well-aimed stone. And they can throw stones a surprising distance, too."

"I'd like to see their blowguns, Uncle. Where are they kept?"

"Come with me and I'll show you," the mission-

ary said as he rose and headed for the farther side
of Tagana's maloka. "Each blowgun is made of a
long straight piece of wood. Usually of a heavy
palm. Bows, clubs and spears are also made of this
elastic wood, but the Tapintins don't use clubs or
spears, as far as I know. Instead of harpooning fish,
for example, they catch them by drugging them, remember?" The missionary motioned toward the
blowguns. "Notice that the pole or staff of those
blowguns is about eight feet long and a couple of
inches in diameter at the end they put in their
mouth when they blow the darts out the other end.
And you can see how the pole tapers down."

"What about the arrows? What are they made
of?" Tom asked.

"Oh, almost any light wood, usually wild cane.
The end of the arrow near the mouthpiece of the
blowgun is usually wrapped in some kind of wild
cotton which grows in a pod on a large tree in Brazil. The other end is sharply pointed and is dipped
in a vegetable poison prepared from various jungle
drugs."

As they walked back and sat down on the jaguar
skin there was still no sign of Tagana.

"You'd have to be strong even to hold the blowgun straight out, let alone steadily, wouldn't you?"
Tom asked.

"Right as rain, my boy," his uncle replied. "But

most Indians who use blowguns are so accurate they can kill small birds at fifty or sixty paces."

"I don't see why the Tapintins need blowguns when they have their bows and arrows," Tom remarked.

"Well, Tom, they use them for different things. Tagana told me his tribe never shoots darts out of blowguns at snakes for fear of making the guns crooked. And he told me that once a blowgun has been used against an alligator it's worthless."

This suggested something to Tom. "If these Tapintins are so superstitious, maybe we can think of some way of scaring them before noon so they won't do anything to Manolo. I don't mean anything silly such as our masquerading as snakes or alligators, but I'll bet there's something we could do!"

"Nine o'clock now," Mr. Jason said glancing at his wrist watch. "I still have hopes that everything will turn out all right, Tom, but time is running out on us. There goes Picasto now to give the signal that will send the Tapintins toward the clearing."

Tom noticed that his uncle was beginning to look more worried than ever. "And look, Uncle," he said gloomily. "Here comes that basket-bearer with the ants. Tagana is walking toward him now. Why can't we ask him again what he is planning? I'm beginning to feel jittery about the whole thing."

"No use, Tom," his uncle said flatly. "He thinks

the sun won't smile if he tells us what is going to happen. I think he makes up some of his superstitions to suit his convenience." As he spoke the Indians who since breakfast had been staining their faces and bodies blue began trooping out of the malokas and shambling toward the clearing. The basket-bearer entered one of the malokas.

"You know, Tom," the missionary said, "I have a hunch that maloka the basket-bearer just entered might be the one where the medicine man lives. Tagana seems to consult his medicine man about his ceremonies, you know. And if the medicine man, or witch doctor really, lives in there maybe we could look around for the radio while the Tapintins are assembled in the clearing. Here comes Tagana again. I reckon he's going to get all dolled up for the ceremony. Come on, Tom, let's take a peek in the witch doctor's maloka and see if he's getting ready, too."

They tried to appear casual as they crossed the village and approached the maloka into which the basket-bearer had disappeared. When they glanced in, the basket-bearer was talking to another Tapintin whose jet-black hair hung down his back in long tresses. Instead of the red or blue stain the Tapintins used, he was stained a bright yellow from head to toe. Even his bark loincloth was a gleaming yellow. The only thing about him that was not yel-

THE GIANT JUNGLE ANTS 149

low was his jet-black hair and his black eyes. In the center of his maloka was a round bamboo cage about six feet high and three feet in diameter. In it was an eagle that was about the same size as the four in the outer camp. And at the eagle's feet was the radio. As they watched, the witch doctor handed the basket-bearer an eagle feather. The latter came out of the maloka and headed for Tagana's maloka.

"Well, Tom, I guess that is that. The medicine man seems to be the only Tapintin who never leaves the village. I guess he's chief watchman as well as adviser to Tagana and witch doctor who cures sick Indians with herbs."

As they returned to Tagana's maloka Tom had a sudden idea. "What would happen, Uncle Leo, if we let those eagles loose that are guarding Manolo?"

"They'd probably fly away. And it would be dangerous to cut them loose with a machete. They would probably attack us or Manolo, who is smeared with monkey fat, remember. And at this stage we still can't do anything to make Tagana mad until we're sure he is planning to harm Manolo."

"But, Uncle, it's getting along toward noon, and yet you seem less worried right now than you were early this morning. Have you something up your sleeve?"

The missionary smiled broadly. "I guess it's mean

of me to keep you in suspense any longer, Tom. I got a bright idea a few minutes ago." He paused as Tagana, now stained blue and replendent in his feathers and bangles, approached them angrily and spoke sharply to Mr. Jason.

"Tagana just told me we'd have to leave the village now and wait for him at the clearing. Let's go. But instead of going to the clearing we're going to make a quick trip out to the *Paloma*."

"What about your idea, Uncle?" Tom asked as they hurried toward the secret exit. "I can see by your expression that it's a beaut."

"We ought to be just about able to get out to the *Paloma* and back," the missionary said half to himself. "But we'll have to hurry. What's the date, did we decide, Tom?" he smiled.

Tom looked puzzled. "July second. But I don't see what that has to do with saving Manolo." Suddenly he brightened. "Gosh, what a dope I've been, Uncle Leo! Why, of course! You mean those firecrackers!"

"Exactly, Thomas Stetson. You gave me the idea when you brought up the date and ways of frightening the Tapintins. This year we're going to celebrate the Fourth of July a couple of days earlier than usual."

CHAPTER FOURTEEN

A FLYING TACKLE

"Thank goodness the skiff is still here, Tom," the missionary said with a sigh when they reached the river's edge. "We would have been sunk if it wasn't."

"Right, Uncle. I'm sure glad we don't have to swim out to the *Paloma* and back through the schools of piranhas. We probably wouldn't have time to swim out and back anyway, and we would have had a tough job keeping the firecrackers dry."

"I was thinking of the piranhas and the time angle, Tom. The *Paloma* has a shallow draft, you know, and if we had to swim out to it I was planning to chug right in against the embankment. But in that case the Tapintins might have heard us and have got suspicious."

"I know one thing," Tom said as he manned the oars. "I'm going to get us a quick snack when we board the *Paloma*. It seems weeks since we've eaten."

"There's some chilled fruit juice in the reefer and some cold meat. One of these days maybe we can eat a meal without rushing," the missionary said. "The sugar cane gives you a quick lift, but we both

151

need some good solid food."

Three buzzards flew off the deck of the launch as they drew alongside. "They're beginning to look as common as pigeons to me," Tom said as he hopped aboard after his uncle. "I'll get out the food while you get the firecrackers if you like."

"Good. First I want to move the launch around the bend in case we want to get away fast. I'll go in close enough so we'll have time to row out to the *Paloma* before the Tapintins have a chance to tote their dugout canoes down and launch them. By the time they do that we ought to be beyond range of their arrows."

It was ten minutes past eleven that morning when Tom headed the skiff back toward the shore in the direction of the attraction post. "I sure feel like a new man after that food, Uncle Leo." He looked up at the blue sky as he rowed. "Not a cloud in sight. We'll have to depend on those rockets and firecrackers, I guess. I just can't wait to see what will happen when they go sizzling and popping around the Indians."

"Well, Tom, if they don't scatter in all directions I'll be surprised," his uncle remarked. "If they don't I want you to run as fast as your legs will carry you to the skiff and streak for the *Paloma*. Then move away and wait for a signal from me for a couple of days. I have always been able to get out of dangerous scrapes with the Indians, but I wouldn't for a minute risk having you depend on their mercy."

"Gosh, Uncle, if anything happened to you I couldn't go away and desert you." Suddenly Tom realized the true danger of their situation. This wasn't fiction any more; this was real—and happening to him.

"Well, let's hope nothing will happen, Tom, but if it does I want you to return to Belem and report what happened to the mission headquarters. I can't risk your life any more than is absolutely necessary. We'll rescue Manolo if it's at all possible, don't worry. Here we are. Let's drag the skiff over into this clump of bushes this time."

"Eleven thirty, Uncle," Tom announced solemnly. "We're nearing the zero hour. Sunday afternoons down on the farm were never like this." Suddenly a worried look appeared on Tom's face as they hid the skiff. "Say, Uncle, if the Tapintins have heard gunshot maybe they will think they're being shot at when the giant firecrackers explode around them. Then won't they rush for their weapons and attack us?"

"I doubt that the Tapintins have ever heard of guns, let alone heard them go off, Tom," the missionary said as they started up the trail. "As far as I know we are the first white men the Tapintins have ever seen. When those sky rockets go whizzing around their heads I'm fairly sure they'll start running back toward the village, scared stiff. They may run amuck, so we had better be careful that they don't trample all over us."

"Have you ever used rockets or firecrackers before, Uncle?" Tom asked.

"Only once, when I first came to Brazil. I was captured by a tribe of Baroyas while I was taking a nap under a tree up near Manaos, the rubber boom town. Some other summer, by the way, we'll take a trip up there. It's roughly a thousand miles from Belem, and I don't think we'll have time to make the trip this summer, since you have to leave for the States by the first of September. It's a dead city now, with rats swarming through the beautiful buildings the rubber kings built. But where was I? Oh, yes, I was telling you how I was captured by the Baroyas. They are cannibals, and they figured I'd make a tasty dish. It was really grim when they tied me up to a tree while they heated some kind of fish oil in a clay pot that was a good six feet high and about ten or twelve feet in circumference. While the oil was heating they went through some kind of ceremonial dance around the pot. The men shook rattles made of human teeth, and they had strings of nutshells on their ankles. The women kept whooping and throwing dirt in my face. All this time I was trying to figure some way of lighting the fuse of a giant firecracker which I had in my pocket. I had several, I remember, just like the ones we have now."

"Jumping Jupiter, Uncle Leo!" Tom exclaimed. "You never told me about that experience. I would have died of fright before they threw me into the pot."

"Well, Tom," the missionary smiled as he looked at his watch, "I figured I'd wait a while before I told you some of the adventures I've had in the past twenty years in Brazil. I didn't want you to have any more of those nightmares. Let's sit down here for a minute. The ceremony won't begin for another half hour or so, so we have plenty of time."

"I don't see how you could get at the firecracker if you were all tied up, Uncle," Tom said as they sat down on the edge of the path.

"That's exactly how it turned out. I tried to keep cool and loosen the bonds, but it was no use. Those vines are tough, as you probably realize by this time. It looked as though the jig was up. What I'm going to tell you now sounds like one of those tall tales, but it's a fact. As they were leading me to the pot to toss me into the boiling oil I managed to sneak out the firecracker. Then I bolted away from the two Baroyas who had me by the arms and ran up to the fire. Before they had time to stop me I lit the fuse, and as about a dozen of the whooping Baroyas rushed me I tossed the firecracker. It made a

terrific racket, and they turned and ran away
screaming. As far as I know they may still be running. Let's hope our Fourth of July celebration is as
successful today. I guess we had better get going
again."

"I wonder," said Tom as they hurried up the trail,
"whether these Tapintins are scared of thunder and
lightning?"

"Not the least bit, Tom. I thought I told you about
that when I talked about the religion of the tribe.
Tagana gravely informed me that when it thunders
the moon and the sun are simply talking to each
other, usually quarreling, because it's usually dark
when there's thunder. And when there is lightning
they are smiling at each other for a second or two.
Well, here we are nearing the clearing. Picasto is
beating his drum. There will be only one more signal, because it's getting close to high noon."

"And we still don't know whether Tagana is planning a wedding or an execution for Manolo," Tom
whispered as his uncle nudged him to be quiet.
"Where are you going?"

"For a while we're going to hide behind this bush.
We don't want to take any chances that Tagana
spots us with our fireworks before the strategic
moment."

Tom crouched beside his uncle and watched the
activity in the clearing intently. "You'll give me the

word when to toss the firecrackers, won't you, Uncle?" he whispered.

"Righto. And at the same time I'll light the fuses of a few skyrockets. If they don't work maybe we'll have to rush at Tagana with some of these Roman candles. There goes the final warning signal."

Tom pulled out his bandanna and mopped the sweat from his brow. "This is really scary, Uncle."

The missionary patted him on the shoulder. "You look excited, Tom, but I don't think you're half as scared as I am."

The assembled Tapintins squatting in a semicircle looked like a blue gigantic ribbon against the green background. As Mr. Jason and Tom had approached the clearing they could be heard chanting, and now, as high noon drew near, the chanting grew louder and more mournful as Tagana strutted toward the center of the clearing and struck a pose with his brawny arms folded. Suddenly the singing ceased as an Indian maiden walked slowly into the clearing from the direction of the village. It was Kalena!

"Well, now we know at last, Uncle Leo!" Tom whispered. "It's going to be a trial of endurance and not an execution. But as you said before, one is almost as bad as the other."

As was the case with the Tapintin maiden at the other wedding ceremony Mr. Jason and Tom had witnessed, Kalena's eyebrows were shaven, and her face was painted a gleaming yellow. Tagana, who had turned toward her when she entered, sat down and ordered her with a gesture to sit down beside him.

"She has no necklace of jaguar teeth," Tom whispered. "I guess Tagana changed the courtship rules all right. But her headdress is made of eagle feathers instead of macaw feathers. It's a lot fancier than the headdress the other bride wore."

Next the basket-bearer entered. As was the case before, he was trailed by another Tapintin who was carrying two straw gloves, which were to be used in the trial of endurance. They were the same gloves that were used before. Tom felt a surge of excitement running through him as Picasto rose and pounded his gourd with the thigh bone of a jaguar. A deep silence followed as Tom held his breath. In a few seconds Manolo would be coming!

Suddenly he appeared, walking slowly, but with head erect. He looked calm and defiant as he approached Tagana and looked straight into his eyes. There was not a flicker of emotion on the chief's face as he stood there with his arms folded across his massive chest. He and Kalena had risen the moment Manolo entered the clearing.

"Manolo certainly has what it takes, Uncle Leo," Tom whispered with tears in his eyes. "He looks sadder than I've ever seen him, but he certainly doesn't look the least bit afraid of Tagana or of the ants. I think the only thing that bothers him is Kalena, and he's ignoring her. I wish we had him on our football team next fall, Uncle. He'd be a whing-ding, I'll bet."

At a word from Tagana, Kalena sat down on the ground and stared straight ahead. She was the first happy-looking Tapintin Tom had ever seen, and it was the first time she looked happy. Picasto came over and sat down beside her. Tagana, who had risen earlier than he had at the previous ceremony, barked a command, and the Indian with the two straw gloves handed one of them to the chief.

"I suppose Kalena thinks she's a knockout, Uncle," Tom whispered. "But that dress she's wearing looks like a tent made of palm leaves. I imagine it's supposed to be a royal outfit."

"Manolo certainly looks small standing there beside Tagana, doesn't he, Tom? Get ready now, and take careful aim. Throw the first giant firecracker right at Tagana if you can."

"Okay, Uncle," Tom said getting ready to go into action. "Just say when."

"As soon as the ants are in the straw glove we let fly, Tom. That will be the most dramatic moment when all eyes are fixed on Manolo and Tagana."

Tom counted the tocandeiras as the chief dropped

them into the glove. "Ten to go," he whispered. "Five—four—three—two—"

"Okay, Tom," the missionary said quietly as he rose. "Light the first fuse and let go."

Tom quickly lit the fuse, rose, and heaved it over the bush. His aim was almost perfect. The firecracker hit Tagana on the chest and bounced off at his feet, just as he was handing the straw glove to Manolo. But the fuse sputtered and went out.

Tom reached for another firecracker frantically. "Gosh, Uncle, I hope I haven't ruined everything. These fuses must be damp. And Manolo is pulling on the glove." As he spoke Tom threw another firecracker at Tagana, who was looking around suspiciously to see where the mysterious firecracker had come from. He was backing away from the first one when the second one Tom threw exploded almost in his face. At the same time the missionary fired the first skyrocket. As Tagana jumped and shrieked the shiny fragments of the rocket burst in the bright sunlight.

"Keep it up, Tom," Mr. Jason said aloud as he fired a second rocket. In the following seconds the clearing was full of the racket of the giant firecrackers and the sizzling skyrockets that whizzed helter-skelter all over the place. The Tapintins, stunned at first, suddenly scrambled to their feet and rushed for the exit leading to the village in a wild panic.

The Firecrackers Startled the Indians

Those who stumbled and fell were trampled by others who rushed forward behind them, and some, unable to get through the milling throng, went crashing through the underbrush surrounding the clearing.

"It's working like a charm, Tom," the missionary exulted. "But I wish Manolo would lower his arm and take off that glove. I don't think he's spotted us yet, but he will."

"But Tagana," Tom shouted. "Look at him. He's screaming, but he's holding his ground. He's rushing around in circles hollering at the Tapintins, but none of them are paying any attention to him." Tom rushed into the clearing as he spoke, and Tagana whirled and glared at him with a look of amazement on his face.

"Quick, Manolo, this way!" Tom shouted.

"Tom, come back here, do you hear?" the missionary called after him. "Tagana will kill you."

Suddenly Tagana wheeled toward the missionary. He advanced with a murderous look in his black eyes, slowly at first, like a cat stalking a rat. Then he filled the air with a gutteral whoop as he rushed angrily at him with the thigh bone of the jaguar that Picasto in his confusion had left behind.

"Run quick, Uncle Leo!" Tom shouted. "He's going to try to kill you." Then Tom rushed at the furious chief without a second's hesitation and flew through the air. He caught Tagana around the knees in a vicious tackle, and the chief fell like a log. In the brief moment the stunned chief lay there stretched out on the ground, Tom hurriedly glanced around for Manolo. He was gone, and the tocandeiras were crawling out of the glove he had flung on the ground.

"Come his minute, Tom, or it may be too late," Mr. Jason shouted as he threw a last firecracker in Tagana's face as the chief rose from the ground shrieking with rage. He backed up for an instant when the firecracker struck him in the face and burned him. He walked around unsteadily rubbing his right eye as Tom and his uncle rushed down the path. As they reached the beach along the river Tom took one fleeting backward glance and saw Tagana charging after them.

"Get into the skiff quick, Uncle, here he comes," Tom gasped as he picked up the oars. The skiff was already skimming over the muddy surface by the time Mr. Jason slumped into the stern seat. He turned, panting, to see what Tagana was doing. When he groaned Tom followed his troubled gaze toward the shore. Tagana had suddenly stopped shaking his fists at them, and now he was racing down the beach toward Manolo who had run in the direction of the attraction post where they had hidden the skiff the day before.

CHAPTER FIFTEEN

A NEW USE FOR HONEY

For a moment Tom let the skiff drift downstream as he rested the oars and watched the Tapintin chief close in on Manolo. Suddenly he began to row furiously toward the shore.

"We've got to save Manolo, Uncle. It may be our last chance," he shouted.

"It's no use, Tom," the missionary panted. "Head for the *Paloma*. It's too late for us to do anything now. Look, Tagana has already caught up with Manolo, and he's dragging him up the trail by the hair. They'll be back in the village by the time we could get ashore and overtake them, and by that time Tagana and his Indians will have their blowguns and bows and arrows in action."

"But he'll surely kill Manolo now, Uncle," Tom said as he changed course and headed for the *Paloma*. "He'll think Manolo spurned his princess daughter, Kalena. He'll never forgive him for that. And he's so mad! He was fit to be tied when that firecracker went off in his face."

"Don't think for a minute that we're giving up on Manolo, Tom," his uncle said as he recovered his

164

breath. "We'll race to Santarem, just as fast as we can. We'll get two or three radios and get back here before Tagana has a chance to kill Manolo by directing the tocandeiras on him."

Tom shook his head wearily. "What a way to die! Eaten alive by ants an inch long!"

"One of these days I'm going to cure those Tapintins of that inhuman custom. Tagana won't carry out the plan until tomorrow at high noon, and that will give us time to get to Santarem and back if we step on it."

"Gee, Uncle, I feel sick when I think of what might happen to Manolo. He's—he's like a brother to me now. He's so rugged, and, boy, does he have courage! Did you notice when he slipped on the glove and the tocandeiras went to work on him? You'd have thought he was pulling on a catcher's mitt or a pair of kid gloves. Not a sign of pain. But his arm was swollen. I could see that from the skiff when Tagana was chasing him. It was almost twice its normal size."

"Speaking of courage, Tom, let me thank you for saving my life. I never saw such a beautiful flying tackle. I don't see how you did it. Tagana weighs a good two hundred to your hundred thirty-five. By the way, you're all smeared with blue stain where you hit him."

"I was just lucky, that's all, Uncle," Tom answered. "I caught him off balance. He really did look funny, though, the way he folded up like an accordion. I guess he never played much football."

"Oh, no. I don't know of any tribe down here that does. I did run across a tribe up around the Orinoco River who played a game something like soccer, but instead of a soccer ball they used a human skull. Well, here we are again. Let's tune up the Diesels and see if we can make it to Santarem and back by tomorrow noon."

Tom's eyes met his uncle's for an instant when they boarded the *Paloma*. "We've simply got to make it, Uncle. We've got to."

"I warn you it won't be easy, Tom," the missionary said gravely as he piloted the launch toward the Tapajos. "From this forlorn spot to Santarem and back it's almost two hundred miles, and we'll be bucking the current on the return trip. We'll need a little luck to make it."

"Here come those Indians again, Uncle," Tom said as he peered through the binoculars at the attraction post. "I can see Tagana and Picasto and a few others shoving off in a big dugout canoe. Tagana doesn't get discouraged very easily, does he? He should know by this time that the *Paloma* is too fast for those dugouts."

"We're in no danger now, I guess, Tom," the missionary said as he slumped into a canvas chair. "I'd better knock on wood, though, I reckon. The *Paloma* could break down or something."

"Gosh, Uncle, the way Tagana feels toward us now, do you think even a radio could scare him?"

"That remains to be seen, Tom. But as far as I can see it's our last chance to rescue Manolo. All I hope is that the radio will weave its magic spell. Especially, if we use two or three of them, and keep one or two out of sight to add to the mystery. There goes Tagana now up to the bow with his arrows. But we're out of range, and if the engines don't stall on us we'll put distance between us all the time."

"I'm getting so used to being chased by Indians in dugouts I don't mind it any more," Tom said as the forward engine coughed and sputtered momentarily, as if to warn him not to get too cocky. His uncle, too, had a worried look for a moment. "Maybe I'd better shush, Uncle," Tom said. "It wouldn't be so funny if the engines conked out on us."

"It certainly wouldn't, Tom." The missionary turned to look at the pursuing Tapintins. "Just as I thought. They're turning back now. They didn't fire a single arrow. Say, Tom, how would you like to go below and whip up some waffles. There's plenty of that prepared mix left, isn't there?"

"What a swell idea! There sure is. After the last few days a good hot mug of cocoa and about eighteen waffles will really hit the spot. I'll have them ready in a jiffy." Tom disappeared into the galley and his uncle continued to gaze at the disappearing figures on shore.

The *Paloma*, throbbing gently, its engines purring like a kitten, swung out of the Tapajos River into the Amazon.

"We're making fairly good time, Tom," the missionary called as he glanced at his watch. "It's only a quarter past two and we're almost a third of the way to Santarem. Come up on deck for a minute if you want to see something interesting."

"What is it, Uncle?" Tom asked eagerly as he rushed to his uncle's side. "What's that I see? It looks like a floating village or something. Look at all the houses and kids playing and the pigs and cows."

"That raft is about three-quarters of a mile long, Tom. Such rafts are common sights on the Amazon, especially during floodtime. In this case a whole village seems to be moving, houses, livestock, children and all."

"There are fourteen shacks and I don't know how many kids chasing around the raft. Where are they going?"

"Perhaps they were flooded out, or maybe they are rubber workers returning from farther up the river."

"Maybe the ants drove them out," Tom said smiling. "Gosh, I smell those waffles burning. I'd better go to look at them."

"I think we're all out of corn syrup, Tom, but there's plenty of honey in the forward cabinet."

"I'll say there is, Uncle. Enough for an army. Three gallons!"

Tom seemed to be thinking hard about something when he brought up the steaming waffles and two mugs of cocoa. "What's up, Tom?" his uncle asked as he accepted a plate of waffles and a mug of cocoa. "You look as if you were a million miles away."

"Oh, I was just daydreaming, I guess, Uncle. Is Santarem an interesting place?"

"Wait until I get my pipe and I'll tell you about it, Tom. Watch the wheel for just a moment." Mr. Jason went below and returned a minute later. He put his pipe in his pocket while he ate his waffles. "Yes, Tom," he began, "Santarem is of special interest to Americans, because after the Civil War many Southerners accepted an invitation of the Emperor of Brazil and settled there. I know several descendants of the original settlers, although most of them have died out, as far as I know." He smiled at Tom as he finished the last sip of cocoa and lit his pipe. Tom was still daydreaming.

"You say some of the Southerners went there after the Civil War, Uncle?" Tom didn't seem as interested in this fact as he normally would have been. "I suppose they all speak Portuguese now.

The descendants of the original settlers, I mean."

Mr. Jason was puzzled by Tom's disinterest. "I'd like to know what's gotten into you, young man," he said as he guided the wheel and puffed contentedly on his pipe. "You seem to have lost your pep. The Emperor I mentioned is Dom Pedro the Second. He was a charming fellow, by the way, who used to walk around the streets of Rio de Janeiro and talk to the folks he met. He visited Boston, incidentally, in the latter part of the last century. Stayed at the old Brunswick Hotel, if I'm not mistaken." Suddenly Mr. Jason interrupted himself and stared worriedly at his nephew. "Tom, tell me, don't you feel well? Why don't you lie down for a few minutes and relax? You've been through a terrible strain these past few days, you know. Why don't you write a few lines to your folks and we can mail the letter in Santarem?"

Suddenly Tom lost his dreamy look. "I was just thinking of something absolutely crazy, Uncle. It's so fantastic I was afraid you'd laugh at me if I mentioned it. But while I was getting the waffles ready this woozy idea kept running through my mind."

"Speak up, my boy," his uncle said, relieved. "After all the clever tricks you've thought up recently you're entitled to at least one crazy idea. In any case, I promise not to laugh. You'll still be batting almost a thousand even if you do strike out one time."

"Well, Uncle, something suddenly struck me when I saw those three big gallon tins of honey. I remembered that you told me not so long ago that the ancient Romans used to smear their enemies with honey and chain them to anthills. And you said the robber barons at Manaos used to do something like that."

"I hope you're not thinking of wasting the honey that way, Tom," the missionary smiled. "It tastes too good on waffles and pancakes."

"Then," Tom continued as if he didn't hear what his uncle was saying, "I thought of the way the Tapintins were trying to kill that poor Pomora captive. You remember how they cut a groove in the tree over his head and waited for the sap to ooze out. The honey reminded me of that sap. And those horrible tocandeiras went after that sap oozing out of the tree the way bees go for clover, right?"

"Righto," the missionary agreed. "But I still don't see what you're driving at, my boy. I wonder if you'd go below and get me a package of matches. I'm all out, and so is my pipe. And then you'd better eat your waffles and drink your cocoa. You have scarcely touched a thing."

Tom returned with the matches and ate his waffles while his uncle watched him fondly without speaking. When he finished the missionary reminded him that he was talking about honey and sap.

"Well, Uncle, this is the crazy idea that has been buzzing through my head. Why can't we save Manolo with those three cans of honey?"

Mr. Jason, puzzled, looked intently at his nephew. "I don't think I follow you, my boy. I don't see any connection between those tins of honey and rescuing Manolo."

Tom seemed hesitant, and a blush heightened the sunburn that days under a tropical sun had given him. "We could use the honey to attract those tocandeiras. I don't mean hundreds or thousands of them, but millions. Tagana and his blooming tribe would be scared out of their wits, but they would have plenty of time to get out of the way of the ants. And meanwhile, we could rescue Manolo."

"I still don't quite see what you're driving at, Tom," the missionary said. "Just how do you plan to use the honey to save Manolo?"

Tom laughed nervously. "Here's where the crazy part comes in, Uncle. I thought we could release the tocandeiras and lure them into the village by dripping honey along the trail from the bamboo tower all the way into the village."

"Hmmmm." Mr. Jason was silent for a moment. "I see now what you're driving at. So that's what all this daydreaming has been about, is it? It sounds fantastic, utterly fantastic. I've never heard of such a thing, but then, come to think of it, I've seen and heard a lot of things the last week or so that have made me sit up and take notice. Take the wheel for a minute, will you, Tom, while I stretch a bit?"

Tom watched his uncle pace back and forth on the tiny deck. Except for the hum of the motors, the silence was complete. They were making good time now. In the hot afternoon sunshine the Amazon River stretched out on one side of the horizon. The shoreline on the other side was a dull green blur.

"I'll take the wheel, now, Tom," the missionary said suddenly. "We're heading back to the Tapintin country. I think you have an idea that might work if we use our heads."

Tom sank down on a deck chair. "Really, Uncle? You think it might work?"

Mr. Jason, as if waking from a dream, smiled and relaxed. "Tom, my boy, I have no idea at the moment as to whether your idea will work, but the more I think of it the better it sounds. I think it beats the radio idea all hollow. Anyway, we're sure going to give your idea a try. Even if we can't lure those tocandeiras up into the village, we can let them out of the bamboo tower. I think that will be enough to give Tagana the jitters.

"But we're still up against our old problem. Time. We'll have to work faster than ever now. Our first problem is to sneak through the village tonight while the Tapintins are sleeping. We might fall right into an ambush while doing that. But if we can make it, and the honey holds out, I don't see why the tocandeiras won't keep coming along the trail. Even if they don't get all the way, the basket-bearer ought to run into them on the way to the tower. And when the poor fellow rushes back into the village and tells Tagana, I have a hunch they will break camp immediately."

"Say, Uncle," Tom said, his curiosity active again, "how does the basket-bearer get the tocandeiras when he goes to the tower? I should think he'd be afraid they'd crawl all over him."

"I imagine, Tom, that he has something in the reed basket that attracts the ants. He probably opens the trap door and lets a number of them crawl into the basket. If you remember that trap door, it's the same shape as the reed basket. The ants could easily fall in, and when the basket-bearer thinks he has enough he simply closes the trap door."

"Well," Tom said, "all I hope now is that we have enough honey. We said it was about a mile and a half from the tower to the village. I should think if we punched a few holes in the top of the cans we could make it if we walked fast. But what about Manolo? We still haven't solved that problem. He may be guarded by the four eagles or Tagana may have him hidden someplace. If we wait until the tocandeiras scare the Tapintins out of their village we may never be able to find Manolo. And if he's guarded by the eagles we have to figure a way of releasing him without any of us being attacked by them."

"Right as usual, Tom. There are plenty of angles." Mr. Jason stopped talking for a few minutes while he thought of some plan of action. "Let's review what we have to do, Tom. First we have to get down to the building where the ants are kept. As we said, it won't be any picnic doing that, because we have to travel at night. And our only route is right through the village."

"Look, Uncle, what if we do that okay. Then let's suppose we find Manolo surrounded by those eagles. In that case we wouldn't have to turn the tocandeiras loose, would we? But how are we going to get rid of the eagles? Suppose they start screaming, or whatever eagles do down here in Brazil?"

"I thought of that problem, too, Tom," his uncle replied. "We have a rifle and a couple of thirty-eights aboard, and I wouldn't hesitate to use them on one or two of those eagles if that was the only way we could think of to save Manolo. But the noise would probably wake the Tapintins. Then it occurred to me that we might sneak up and grab a couple of their blowguns, but neither of us has had any experience with them, so I'm afraid they're out. The same goes for the bows and arrows. I don't think I could hit a barn door at ten feet, and you have never used a bow and arrow, either. It's a tough problem, however you look at it." Mr. Jason sighed deeply and worriedly ran a hand through his hair.

"Well, Uncle, I thought of one plan, but I don't think it would work, because I'm afraid the eagles would scream or squawk while we were trying to work it. I thought we might climb that tree which is near the four eagles. Then I could crawl out on the limb right over Manolo's head and toss him a rope. I'd pull him up and he could climb onto the limb and shinny down the tree. But the eagles would be so excited, probably, they'd make a terrific racket."

"I think you're right. We'd have to keep the eagles busy in some way. One idea I had was to take along a few pounds of hamburger, and while the birds were gulping it down Manolo could swish by them before they could get at him. I have an idea they would be so busy with the hamburger they'd ignore Manolo for the moment."

"That was my other idea, Uncle Leo. We have ten or twelve pounds of hamburger left in the deep freeze. That should be enough, don't you think?" Tom's voice rose excitedly when he realized they had found a possible escape for Manolo.

herbs. If he did, and Manolo is in a deep slumber, it will be a job for us to carry him if we can't wake him up. Especially, with millions of ants milling around."

CHAPTER SIXTEEN

THE WITCH DOCTOR SLEEPS

"Everything is ready now, Uncle Leo," Tom said half an hour later. "I have the meat in four separate packages, one for each eagle. I put an extra mosquito net in my knapsack just in case we might need it for something. Also, a rope, which may come in handy."

"I'll check my gear, too," the missionary said. "Let's see, machete, mosquito net, flashlight, some sugar cane to nibble on to pep us up. Tom, why don't we take along half a dozen cans of K-rations in case we have to stay in the jungle longer than we expect?"

"A great idea, Uncle," Tom said. "I wish we had taken some along for our last jungle adventure. And I'm glad you reminded me about my machete. While I'm below I'll feed Ozzy. That poor little ocelot sure has been on her own lately. But I'll make up for all that now by giving her some hamburger."

"And while you're below you'd better put a new bulb in the clothes cabinet. I noticed that the bulb had gone out, and if we don't keep it hot in there our clothes may get mildewed."